"Let's change the rules of our partnership."

Blake continued quickly, "We agreed that our relationship would be platonic, lasting as long as..."

"My father lives," Sapphire finished for him.

"I'm suggesting that we lift that self-imposed ban and make our marriage real in every sense of the word, to be..."

"Set aside when we no longer desire each other?"

"Is that what you want?"

Perhaps the fact that Miranda was now married broke Blake's personal code of behavior, Sapphire didn't know. But it was pride alone that kept her from crying out that she wanted to share his life and his bed forever. "Yes," she said finally.

"Very well then. For as long as our desire lasts, so does our marriage."

Books by Penny Jordan

HARLEQUIN PRESENTS

477—TIGER MAN
484—MARRIAGE WITHOUT LOVE
489—LONG COLD WINTER
508—NORTHERN SUNSET
517—BLACKMAIL
519—THE CAGED TIGER
537—DAUGHTER OF HASSAN
553—AN UNBROKEN MARRIAGE
562—BOUGHT WITH HIS NAME
569—ESCAPE FROM DESIRE
584—THE FLAWED MARRIAGE
591—PHANTOM MARRIAGE
602—RESCUE OPERATION
609—DESIRE'S CAPTIVE
618—A SUDDEN ENGAGEMENT
633—PASSIONATE PROTECTION
641—ISLAND OF THE DAWN
650—SAVAGE ATONEMENT
667—FORGOTTEN PASSION
706—SHADOW MARRIAGE
713—THE INWARD STORM
728—RESPONSE
738—WANTING
746—DARKER SIDE OF DESIRE
755—RULES OF THE GAME
761—CAMPAIGN FOR LOVING
770—WHAT YOU MADE ME
785—THE ONLY ONE
794—THE FRIENDSHIP BARRIER
809—THE SIX-MONTH MARRIAGE

These books may be available at your local bookseller.

Don't miss any of our special offers. Write to us at the following address for information on our newest releases.

Harlequin Reader Service
P.O. Box 52040, Phoenix, AZ 85072-2040
Canadian address: P.O. Box 2800, Postal Station A,
5170 Yonge St., Willowdale, Ont. M2N 6J3

PENNY JORDAN

the six-month marriage

Harlequin Books

TORONTO • NEW YORK • LONDON
AMSTERDAM • PARIS • SYDNEY • HAMBURG
STOCKHOLM • ATHENS • TOKYO • MILAN

Harlequin Presents first edition August 1985
ISBN 0-373-10809-5

Original hardcover edition published in 1985
by Mills & Boon Limited

CHAPTER ONE

'Sapphire, you haven't heard a word I've said. What's wrong?' Alan asked her.

The densely blue, dark lashed eyes that were the reason for Sapphire's unusual name turned in his direction, her brief smile not totally hiding the concern in their dark blue depths.

'I've had a letter from home this morning, and apparently my father isn't well.'

'Home?' Alan gave her a strange look. 'Funny, that's the first time I've heard you call it that in the four years that you've worked for me. Before it's always been Grassingham.'

Frowning slightly, Sapphire left her desk, pacing restlessly. It was true that in the four years she had worked in London she had tried to wipe her memory clean of as much of the past as she could, and that included any foolishly sentimental references to the border village where she had grown up as 'home', but in times of crisis, mental conditioning, no matter how thorough, was often forgotten. Her father confined to bed and likely to remain a semi-invalid for the rest of his life!

Unconsciously she stopped pacing and stared through the large window of her office, but instead of seeing the vista of office blocks and busy London streets all she could see was her childhood home; the farm which had belonged to many generations of Bells and which had been handed

down from father to son from the time of
Elizabeth the First. But of course *her* father had
no son to carry on farming the land he loved, that
was why... Sapphire gnawed worriedly at her
bottom lip. In the Borders people adapted to
social changes very slowly. Those who lived there
had a deeply ingrained suspicion of 'new ideas',
but had she wanted to do so, she knew that her
father would have encouraged her to undertake
the agricultural degree needed to successfully run a
farm the size of Flaws. However, although she had
grown up on the farm she had had no desire to
take over from her father.

Flaws valley was one of the most fertile in the
area, and should her father decide to sell, there
would be no shortage of buyers. But how *could* he
sell? It would break his heart. After her mother
had left him he had devoted himself exclusively to
the farm and to her. Her mother. Sapphire sighed.
She could barely remember her now, although she
knew that she looked very much like her.

It was from her American mother that she had
inherited her wheat blonde hair and long lithe
body, both of which were viewed with a touch of
scorn in the Borders.

'She's the looks and temperament of a race
horse,' one neighbour had once commented
scornfully to her father, 'but what you need for
these valleys is a sturdy pony.'

Acutely sensitive, Sapphire had grown up
knowing that the valley disapproved of her
mother. She had been flighty; she had been
foreign; but worst of all she had been beautiful
with no other purpose in life but to *be* beautiful.
Although she had been fiercely partisan on her

father's behalf as a child—after all she too had shared his sense of rejection, for when her mother left with her lover there had been no question of taking a four-year-old child with her—older now herself Sapphire could understand how the valley had stifled and finally broken a woman like her mother, until there had been nothing left for her other than flight.

A farmer's hours were long hours, and her mother had craved parties and entertainment, whereas all her father wanted to do in the evenings was to relax. Her mother was dead now, killed in a car accident in California, and she. . . Despite the warmth of her centrally heated office Sapphire shivered. She knew she had never been wholly accepted by her peers in the valley and that was why she had responded so hungrily to whatever scraps of attention she had been given. A bitter smile curved her mouth and she looked up to find Alan watching her worriedly.

Dear Alan. Their relationship was such a comfortable one. She enjoyed working for him, and after the emotional minefields she had left behind her when she left the valley, his calm affection made her feel secure and relaxed. Their friends looked on them as an established couple although as yet they weren't lovers, which suited Sapphire very well. She wasn't sure if she was strong enough yet to involve herself too intimately with another human being. As she knew all too well, intimacy brought both pleasure and pain and her fear of that pain was still stronger than her need of its pleasure. Divorce was like that, so other people who had been through the same thing told her. Along with the self-doubts and anguish ran a deep current of inner dread of commitment.

'Alan, I'm afraid I'm going to have to ask for time off so that I can go and see my father.'

'Of course. If we weren't so busy, I'd drive you up there myself. How long do you think you'll need? We've got quite a lot to get through before the end of the month and we're away for all of March.'

Alan's small import business had been very successful the previous year and he was rewarding himself and Sapphire with a month's holiday cruising round the Caribbean; an idyll which Sapphire sensed would culminate in them becoming lovers. Without saying so outright Alan had intimated that he wanted to marry her. Her father seemed to have sensed it too because in his last letter to her he had teased her about the 'intentions' of this man she wrote about so often. She had written back, saying that they were 'strictly honourable'.

'Don't worry too much.' Alan comforted, misunderstanding the reason for her brief frown. 'If your father's well enough to write. . .'

'He isn't.' Sapphire cut in, her frown deepening.

'Then who was the letter from?'

'Blake.' Sapphire told him brittly.

When Alan's eyebrows rose, she added defensively, 'He and my father are very close. His land runs next to Flaws Farm, and his family have been there nearly as long as ours. In fact the first Sefton to settle there was a border reiver—a supporter of Mary Queen of Scots, who according to local rumour managed to charm Elizabeth enough to be pardoned.'

'Do you still think about him?'

For a moment the quiet question threw her. She knew quite well who the 'him' Alan referred to was, and her face paled slightly under her skilful application of makeup. 'Blake?' she asked lightly, adopting the casual tone she always used when anyone asked her about her ex-husband. 'We were married when I was eighteen and we parted six months later. I don't think about him any more than I have to, Alan. He was twenty-six when we were married, and unlike me he knew exactly what he was doing.'

'I hardly recognise you when you talk about him,' Alan murmured coming across to touch her comfortingly. 'Your voice goes so cold. . .'

'Perhaps because when I talk about Blake that's how I feel; terribly cold, and very, very old. Our marriage was a complete disaster. Blake was unfaithful to me right from the start. The only reason he married me was because he wanted Flaws' land, but I was too besotted—too adolescently infatuated with him to see that. I thought he loved me, and discovering that he didn't. . .'

She shuddered, unable to go any further; unable to explain even now the terrible sense of disillusionment and betrayal she had experienced when she discovered the truth about her marriage. It was four years since she had last seen Blake— and four years since she had last seen her father, she reminded herself, mainly because she had refused to go home and risk meeting Blake, and her father had been too busy with the farm to come to London and see her. And now this morning she had received Blake's letter, telling her about the pneumonia that had confined her father to bed.

A terrible ache spread through her body. It hurt to know that her father had been so ill and she had not known. He had not written or phoned to tell her. No, that had been left up to Blake, with the curt p.s. to his letter that he thought she should come home. 'Although he doesn't say so, I know your father wants to see you,' he had written in the decisive, black script that was so familiar to her— familiar because of that other time she had seen it; the day she had discovered the love letter he had written to one of his other women. The tight ball of pain inside her chest expanded and threatened to explode, but she willed it not to. She had already endured all that; she wasn't going to allow it to return. There was a limit to the extent of mental agony anyone could be expected to suffer, and she had surely suffered more than her share, learning in the space of six months that the husband she worshipped had married her simply because he wanted her father's land, and that he had not even respected their marriage vows for a week of that marriage. While he left her untouched save for the brief kiss he gave her each morning as he left the farm, he had been making love to other women; women to whom he wrote intensely passionate love letters—love letters that had made her ache with longing; with pain; with jealousy. Even now she could still taste the bitterness of that anguished agony. She had gone straight from discovering the letters to her father, complaining that she did not believe that Blake loved her. Not even to him could she confide what she had found, and when he questioned her, she had simply told him of Blake's preoccupation; of his darkly sombre moods, of the little time he spent with her.

'I don't know why he married me,' she had cried despairingly, and her father taking pity on her had explained how worried he had been about the future of the farm once he was gone, and how he and Blake had agreed on their marriage, which was more the marriage of two parcels of land than two human beings.

She hadn't told her father about discovering Blake's infidelities, and for the first time in her life she had truly appreciated how her mother must have felt. From that to making the decision to leave Flaws valley had been a very short step. Blake had been away at the time buying a new ram and she vividly remembered, tiptoeing downstairs with her suitcase and out through the large flagged kitchen, leaving a note for him on the table. In it she had said simply that she no longer wanted to be married to him. Her pride wouldn't let her write anything else, and certainly nothing about Miranda Scott who had been one of Blake's regular girlfriends before he started dating her. She had bumped into Miranda in the library and the other girl had eyed her tauntingly as she told her about the night she had spent with Blake the previous week. Blake had told her that he was buying fresh stock and that he would have to stay in the Cotswolds overnight.

She had asked if she could go with him, thinking that away from the farm she might find it easier to talk to him about her unhappiness with their marriage. In the months leading up to it she had been thrilled by the way he kissed and caressed her and had looked forward eagerly to their wedding night, but she had spent it alone as she had all the nights that followed, and that had been one of the

most galling things of all, the fact that her
husband didn't find her attractive enough to want
to make love to her.

But he found Miranda attractive—so attractive
that he had taken her to the Cotswolds with him.

At first when she reached London she had used
an assumed name, terrified that Blake would try to
find her, and terrified that if he did, she wouldn't
have the pride or strength of will to refuse to go
back to him. Not that she was under any illusions
any more that he wanted her. No, he wanted her
father's land!

Those first six months in London had been
bitterly lonely. She had drawn all her money out
of her bank account before leaving the valley and
there had been enough to support her for the first
three months while she took a secretarial course.
Her first job she had hated, but then she had
found her present job with Alan. She had also
enough confidence by then to find herself a
solicitor. She could have had her marriage
annulled—after all it had never been consummated—but she hadn't wanted anyone to know
the humiliating truth—that her husband hadn't
found her attractive enough to want to consum-
mate it—so instead she had patiently waited out
the statutory time before suing for divorce. She
had half expected, even then, some reaction from
Blake but there had been none and their divorce
had become final just five months ago.

Sapphire had been in London seven months
before she wrote to her father. Before leaving the
valley she had posted a letter to him telling him
she was leaving Blake, and saying that nothing
would make her come back.

With hindsight she could see how worried her father must have been when he didn't hear from her, but at the time she had been so concerned with protecting herself both from Blake and from her own treacherous emotions that she hadn't been able to think past them.

'Do you plan to drive North, or will you go by train?'

Jerked out of her reverie by Alan's voice Sapphire forced herself to concentrate. 'I'll drive,' she told him. 'There isn't a direct train service and driving will save time.'

'Then you'd better take my car,' Alan told her calmly, 'I wouldn't feel happy about you driving so far in yours.'

It was true that her battered VW had seen better times, and Sapphire felt the same warm glow she always experienced when Alan was so thoughtful. Being married to him would be like being wrapped in insulating fibre; protected. Protected from what? From her past? From her foolish adolescent craving for the love of a man who was simply using her? That's all over now, Sapphire told herself sharply. Blake means nothing to me now. Nothing at all.

'Look, why don't you go home now and get yourself organised,' Alan suggested. 'You're too strung up to be much use here, and you'll need an early start in the morning. Here are my car keys.' He frowned. 'No, I'll go and fill the tank up first. That should be enough to get you all the way there. And when you arrive, 'phone me won't you? I wish there was some way I could come with you.'

'Dear Alan.' Sapphire rested her head against

his shoulder—a rare expression of physical affection for her. 'You're so good to me.'

'Because you're worth being good to,' Alan retorted gruffly. Expressions of emotions always embarrassed him, and as she withdrew from him Sapphire wondered why she should remember so clearly the sensual seduction of the words Blake had written; words which still had the power to move her even now, and yet Blake too was a man of few words, but then unlike Alan, Blake's words were always pithy and to the point. Blake deplored waste of any kind; a true Sefton; and yet there was something about him that had always attracted and yet frightened her. He had spent several years in the army after leaving university. Perhaps that was where he had developed that hard veneer that was so difficult to get past. Sapphire knew that he had been posted to Northern Ireland, and yet his experiences there were something he never did discuss—not even with her father. When she had commented on it once, her father had simply said, 'There are some things a man can't endure to remember, and so for the sake of his sanity he forgets them. War is one of them.'

An hour later, gripping the cord of the telephone receiver as she waited for someone to answer the 'phone, she felt her stomach muscles contract with tension. According to Blake's letter her father didn't know he had written, so she must try to pretend that she knew nothing of his illness. The ringing seemed to last for ever, and for one dreadful moment Sapphire pictured her father lying in bed, listening to the demanding sound, too ill to do anything about it, but then the receiver was lifted, the ringing abruptly cut off. Relief made her voice hesitantly husky, 'Dad, it's Sapphire.'

The cool male voice, edged with taunting mockery, wasn't her father's, and the tiny hairs on her arm stood up in prehensile alarm as she recognised it.

'Blake?'

'How very flattering that you should recognise my voice so quickly after all this time.'

'They say people always remember anything connected with acute trauma,' Sapphire snapped sharply. 'Blake, I've got your letter. My father, how is he?'

'Why don't you come home and see for yourself, or are you still running scared?'

'What of? You? Of course I'm coming h ... back, but I can hardly arrive without warning Dad to expect me.'

'Very thoughtful. Giving him time to kill the fatted calf is that it? I take it you're coming alone,' he added, before she could respond. 'Flaws Farm only has three bedrooms remember; your father's in one, his housekeeper's in the other, and I'm sure I don't need to tell you how the valley will feel about one of its daughters openly co-habiting with a man she isn't married to—to say nothing of your father's feelings.'

Gritting her teeth Sapphire responded. 'I'm coming alone, but only because Alan couldn't make it. Now may I please speak to my father?'

It was only when Blake put the receiver down that she realised she hadn't asked him what he was doing at Flaws Farm. He had sounded very much at home, and she bit worriedly at her bottom lip.

She had forgotten how freely Blake was used to coming and going in her old home, and if she was forced to endure the constant sight of him how would it affect the calm control she had sheltered behind for so long?

It won't affect it at all, she told herself angrily. Why should it? Blake had effectively killed whatever feelings she had had for him—and they had only been infatuation—a very deep and intense infatuation agreed, but infatuation nevertheless. . .

Five minutes later she was speaking to her father, unable to stop the weak tears rolling down her face. Normally they only rang one another at Christmas and birthdays, and it shocked her to hear the hesitancy in his voice.

'Blake tells me you intend paying us a visit?'

'If you've got room for me. I hear you've got a housekeeper?' Sapphire responded drily.

'Yes, Mary Henderson. You probably remember her from the old days. She used to nurse at the local hospital. She was widowed a couple of years ago, and her husband left a lot of debts, so she had to sell her house and look for a job. Blake recommended her to me. This is still your home Sapphire,' he added in a different voice. 'There's always a room for you here.'

Without saying it he was making her aware of all the times she should have gone home and hadn't, because she hadn't been able to conquer her weakness; her fear of meeting Blake, and discovering that she wasn't as strong as she had believed. What was she really frightened of though? Blake seducing her? Hardly likely—after all he hadn't wanted her when they were married, so why should he want her now?

'Expect me late tomorrow evening,' Sapphire told him. 'Alan's lending me his car, because he doesn't think my old VW is reliable enough.' For some reason Sapphire found the silence that followed oddly disconcerting.

'You'd better use the top road,' her father said at last. 'They've been doing some roadworks on the other one and there've been traffic jams all week just this side of Hawick.'

Mentally revising her plans, Sapphire said her goodbyes. She had planned to drive up the M6 to Carlisle and then take the A7 through Hawick and Jedburgh, rather than using the 'top road' which was shorter but which meant driving along the narrow winding road which crossed and re-crossed the Cheviots.

That night, too wide-awake to sleep, she acknowledged that hearing Blake's voice had disturbed her—dangerously so. The sound of it brought back memories she had struggled to suppress; herself at fourteen watching with shy adulation while Blake worked. Fresh from university he had seemed like a god from Olympus to her and she had dogged his footsteps, hanging on to his every word. Was it then that he had decided to marry her? It was certainly then that he had started to put into practice the modern farming techniques he had learned partially at university and partially during his working holidays in New Zealand into force. Perhap's it was also then that he had first cast covetous eyes on Flaws Farm and mentally calculated the benefits to himself of owning its rich acres in addition to his own. She would never know, but certainly he had been kind and patient with her, carefully answering all her shy questions, tactfully ignoring her blushes and coltish clumsiness. She remembered practically falling off her pony one day straight into his arms, and how she had felt when they closed round her, the steady beat of his heart thumping into her thin chest. From that day on she had started to weave the fantasies about him that had taken her blissfully into their marriage.

At eighteen she had known very little of the world—had only travelled as far as Edinburgh and Newcastle and had certainly not got the sophistication to match Blake. He had left the valley when she was fifteen to join the army and had returned two years later the same and yet different; harder, even more sure of himself and possessed of a dangerous tension that sent frissons of awareness coursing over her skin whenever he looked at her.

The Christmas she was seventeen he had kissed her properly for the first time in the large living room of Sefton House—the large rambling building his great-grandfather had built when a fire had gutted the old farmhouse. There had been a crowd of people there attending a Boxing Day party and someone had produced a sprig of mistletoe. Even now she could vividly remember the mixture of anticipation and dread with which she had awaited Blake's kiss. She had known he *would* kiss her. He had kissed all the other girls, but the kiss he gave her was different, or so she had told herself at the time. Her first 'grown-up' kiss; the first time she had experienced the potency of sexual desire. His mouth had been firm and warm, his lips teasing hers, his tongue probing them apart.

Restlessly, Sapphire sat up in bed, punching

her pillow. She must get some sleep if she was going to be fresh for her drive tomorrow. No doubt if Blake were to kiss her now she would discover that his kisses were nothing like as arousing as she remembered. She had been an impressionable seventeen-year-old to his twenty-five already halfway to worshipping him, and during the brief spring days he had cashed in on that adoration, until by summer he filled her every thought. He had proposed to her one hot summer's day beside the stream that divided Sefton and Bell land. Blake had wanted to swim, she remembered, in the deep pool formed by the waterfall that cascaded into it. She had objected that she hadn't brought her suit and Blake had laughed at her, saying that neither had he. She had trembled as revealingly as a stalk of wheat before the reaper, not troubling to hide her reaction. He had pulled her to him, kissing her; caressing her with what she had naively taken to be barely restrained passion. God how ridiculous she must have seemed. Blake's actions couldn't have been more calculated had they been programmed by computer, and whatever passion there had been had been for her father's lands and nothing else.

'Damn Blake, this is all his fault,' Sapphire muttered direfully the next morning, as she ate a hurriedly prepared breakfast. Ten o'clock already, and she had hoped to leave at eight, but she hadn't been able to get to sleep until the early hours and then when she had done she had slept restlessly, dreaming of Blake, and of herself as they had been. Now this morning there was a strange ache in the region of her heart. She couldn't mourn a love she had never had, she reminded herself as she had done so often during those first agonising months in London, and Blake had never loved her. It had been hard to accept that, but best in the long run. She had once suffered from the delusion that Blake loved her and the penalty she had paid for that folly had warned her against the folly of doing so again.

It was eleven o'clock before she finally managed to leave. The day was crisp and cold, a weak sun breaking through the clouds. February had always been one of her least favourite months—Christmas long forgotten and Spring still so far away, and she was looking forward to her holiday. There was something faintly decadent about going to the Caribbean in March.

A John Williams tape kept her company until she was clear of the City. Blake had had very catholic tastes in music and in books, but it was only since coming to London that her own tastes had developed. Music was a key that unlocked human emotions she thought as she slowed down to turn the tape over. Alan's BMW was his pride and joy, and although she appreciated his thoughtfulness in lending it to her, she was slightly apprehensive with it.

She had planned to stop for lunch somewhere round Manchester, but oversleeping had altered her schedule, and she glanced at her watch as she travelled north and decided instead to press on to Carlisle and stop there.

She found a pleasant looking pub a few miles off the motorway and pulled up into the car park, easing her tired body out of the car. As she walked in the bar she felt the sudden silence descending on the room, and suppressed a wry grimace. She had forgotten how very conservative northern men were. Even now very few women up here entered pubs alone, but she shrugged aside the sudden feeling of uncertainty and instead headed for the bar, breathing in the appetising smell of cooking food.

The menu when she asked for it proved to be surprisingly varied. She ordered lasagne and retreated to a small corner table to wait for it to be served. While she waited she studied the people around her; mostly groups of men, standing by the bar while their womenfolk sat round the tables. So much for women's lib, she thought drily, watching them. If she had stayed at home she could well have been one of these women. And yet they seemed quite happy; they were fashionably dressed and from the snatches of conversation she caught even the married ones seemed to have jobs, which to judge from their comments they enjoyed.

A chirpy barmaid brought the lasagne and the coffee she had ordered. The pasta was mouth-wateringly delicious. She hadn't realised how hungry she had been, Sapphire reflected as she drank her coffee, reluctant to leave the warmth of the pub for the raw cold of the February night outside, but she was already late. At last, reluctantly, she got up and made her way to the car, unaware of the way several pairs of male eyes followed her tall, lithe body. She had dressed comfortably for the journey, copper coloured cords toning with a coffee and copper sweater, flat-heeled ankle boots in soft suede completing her outfit. She had always worn her hair long, but in London she had found a hairdresser who cared about the condition of his clients' hair and now hers shone with health, curving sleekly down on to her shoulders.

The BMW started first time, its powerful lights picking out the faint wisps of mist drifting down from the hills. Living in London insulated one from the elements, Sapphire thought, shivering as she drove out of the car park, and switched the car heater on to boost. She had to concentrate carefully on the road so that she didn't miss the turning which would take her on to the 'top road' and she exhaled faintly with relief when she found it. The mist had grown thicker, condensation making it necessary for her to switch on the windscreen wipers, the BMW's engine started to whine slightly as the road climbed. She had forgotten how quickly this road rose; the Cheviots were gentle hills compared with some, but they still rose to quite a height. It was an eerie sensation being completely alone on this empty stretch of road, her lights the only ones to illuminate the darkness of the bare hills. Here and there her headlights picked out patches of snow and then visibility would be obscured by the mist that seemed to waft nebulously around her.

Despite the heater she felt quite cold. Nerves, she told herself staunchly, automatically checking her speed as the mist started to thicken. Now she noticed with dismay the patches of mist were longer, and much, much, denser. In fact they weren't mist at all, but honest-to-God fog. It was freezing as well. She had thought it might be several miles back when she felt so cold, but now she felt the BMW's front wheels slide slightly, and tried not to panic. The BMW had automatic transmission, but there was a lower gear and she dropped into it, biting her lip as she crawled down a steep hill.

Nine o'clock! Her father would be wondering where on earth she was. Why hadn't she rung him from the pub and told him she was likely to be late? It was useless now chastising herself for not anticipating adverse weather conditions. One of the first things she had learned as a child was not to trust the Border weather, but she had lived in London for so long that she had forgotten. She tensed as the BMW slid sickeningly round a sharp bend, blessing the fact that she had the road to herself. She ought never to have come this way. The traffic jams in Hawick would have been much preferable to this.

How many miles had she come? It felt like hundreds, but it was probably barely ten, and it was at least thirty to Flaws valley. She hadn't reached the highest part of the road yet either.

Trying not to panic Sapphire concentrated on the road, watching the thick grey film in front of her until her eyes ached. The road had no central markings; no cat's eyes, and on several occasions she felt the change in camber, warning her that she was veering too much to one side or the other.

It was a terrible, nightmare drive, and when the road finally peaked, and she was out above the fog, she trembled with relief. Snow still lined the road, this high up, and the tarmac surface shone dull grey with frost. She was over halfway there now.

Gradually the road started to drop down until she was back into the fog. In her relief to be over the top she had forgotten the sharpness of the bends on the downward road. Several times she felt the BMW slide as she cornered, and each time she prayed she wouldn't panic, refusing to give in to the temptation to brake, trying to steer the car into and then out of the skid.

When she eventually saw the sign for Flaws Valley she could hardly believe her own eyes! Elation made her weak with relief as her senses relayed to her the familiarity of the straight road through the village. Everything was in darkness. People in Flaws village kept early hours. Most of them worked on the land and there was nothing in the village to keep them out late at night. And yet as she remembered it she had never suffered from boredom as a teenager; there had always been plenty to do. Harvest Festivals; Christmas parties and pantomime; summer haymaking; barbecues. Lost in her thoughts she turned instinctively into the road that ran past Blake's farm and then on to her father's. A wall loomed up in front of her with shocking suddenness, emerging from the mist, making her brake instinctively. She felt the car skid almost immediately, wrenching the wheel round in a desperate effort to avoid the wall. She felt the sudden lurch as the car left the road and came to rest with its front wheels in the ditch. Her head hit the windscreen, the pull of her seatbelt winding her. The shock of her accident robbed her of the ability to do anything but grasp the wheel and shiver. The front of the car had hit the wall. She had heard the dull screech of metal against stone.

She must get out of the car. Shakily she switched off the ignition and freed herself from her seatbelt. Her forehead felt cold and damp. She touched it, staring foolishly at the sticky red blood staining her fingers as she pulled them away. She had cut herself, but she could move, albeit very shakily. The car door opened easily and she stepped out on to the road, shuddering with shock and cold as the freezing air hit her. What next? She was approximately five miles from home and two from the village. Blake's house was half a mile up the road, but she couldn't go there. The village was her best bet. Shakily she started out, only to tense as she heard the sound of another vehicle travelling down the road. From the sound of it, it was being driven with far more assurance than she had possessed. Its driver seemed to know no fear of the fog or the ice. Instinctively Sapphire stepped back off the road, wincing slightly as she realised she must have twisted her ankle against the pedals. Bright headlights pierced the fog, and she recognised the unmistakeable shape of a Land Rover. It stopped abruptly by the BMW and the engine was cut. The driver's door jerked open and a man jumped out. Tall and lean, his long legs were encased in worn jeans, a thick navy jumper covering the top half of his body. He walked towards the BMW and then stopped, lifting his head, listening as though he sensed something.

'Sapphire?'

Her heart thumping, her body tense Sapphire waited. She had known him immediately, and was shaken by her childish desire to keep silent; to run from him.

'Sapphire?' He called her name again and then cursed under his breath.

She was being stupid, Sapphire told herself, and

added to that she was beginning to feel distinctly odd. Blake's shadowy figure seemed to shift in patterns of mist, the sound of her own heartbeats one moment loud the next very faint.

'Blake ... over here.' How weak her voice sounded but he heard it. He came towards her with the certainty of a man who knows his way blindfolded. As he got closer Sapphire could see the droplets of moisture clinging to his dark hair. His face was tanned, his eyes the same disturbing gold she remembered so vividly. He was so close to her now that she could feel his breath against her skin.

'So you decided to come after all.' He voice was the same; that slight mocking drawl which had once so fascinated her was still there. 'I began to think you'd chickened out... What's the boy-friend going to say when he knows you've ruined his car?'

Not one word of concern for her. Not one solicitous phrase; not one comforting touch ... nothing. She knew she had to say something, but all she could manage was a pitiful sound like a weak kitten, her senses acutely attuned to everything about him. She could feel the leashed energy emanating from his body; smell the clean cold scent of his skin. She shivered feeling reality recede and darkness wash over her. As she slid forward she felt Blake's arms catch and then lift her.

'Well, well,' he murmured laconically. 'Here you are back in my arms. The last place you swore you'd ever be again. Remember?'

She tried to tell him that she had never been properly in his arms; that she had never known them as those of a lover, but it was too much effort. It was simpler by far to close her eyes and absorb the delicious warmth emanating from his body, letting her senses desert her.

CHAPTER TWO

'COME on Sapphire, the shock can't have been that great.' The coolly mocking words broke against her senses like tiny darts of ice as she started to come round. She was sitting in a chair in the kitchen of Sefton House, and that chair was drawn up to the warmth of the open fire. The flames should have comforted her, but they weren't powerful enough to penetrate the chill of Blake's contempt. 'Flaws Valley females don't go round fainting at the first hint of adversity,' he taunted, watching her with a cynical smile. 'That's a London trick you've learned. Or was your faint simply a way of avoiding the unpalatable fact of our meeting?'

She had forgotten this side of him; this dangerous cynical side that could maim and destroy.

'I knew when I came up here that we were bound to meet, Blake.' She was proud of her composure, of the way she was able to meet the golden eyes. 'My faint was caused simply by shock—I hadn't expected the weather to be so bad.' She glanced round the kitchen, meticulously avoiding looking directly at him. She lifted her hand to touch her aching temple, relieved to discover the cut had healed. 'Don't worry,' Blake tormented, 'it's only a scratch!'

She had either forgotten or never fully realised, the intensity of the masculine aura he carried around him. It seemed to fill the large kitchen, dominantly. Droplets of moisture clung to the thick wool of his sweater, his hair thick and dark where it met the collar. His face and hands were tanned, his face leaner than she remembered, the proud hard-boned Celtic features clearly discernible.

The gold eyes flickered and Sapphire tensed, realising that she had been staring. 'What's the matter?' Blake taunted, 'Having second thoughts? Wishing you hadn't run out on me?'

'No.' Her denial came too quickly; too fervently; and she tensed beneath the anger she saw simmering in his eyes. The kitchen was immaculately clean; Blake had always been a tidy man but Sapphire sensed a woman's presence in the room.

'Do you live here alone?'

She cursed herself for asking the impulsive question when she saw his dark eyebrows lift.

'Now why should that interest you? As a matter of fact I do,' he added carelessly, 'although sometimes Molly stays over if it's been a particularly long day.'

'Molly?' She hoped her voice sounded disinterested, but she daren't take the risk of looking at Blake. What was the matter with her? She had been the one to leave Blake; she had been the one to sue for a divorce, so why should she feel so distressed now on learning that there might possibly be someone else in his life? After all he had never loved her. Never made any pretence of loving her. But she had loved him ... so much that she could still feel the echoes of that old pain, but echoes were all they were. She no longer loved

Blake, she had put all that behind her when she
left the valley.

'Molly Jessop,' Blake elucidated laconically,
'You probably remember her as Molly Sutcliffe.
She married Will Jessop, but he was killed in a car
accident just after you left. Molly looks after the
house for me; she also helps out with the office
work.'

Molly Sutcliffe. Oh yes, Sapphire remembered
her. Molly had been one of Blake's girlfriends in
the old days. Five years older than Sapphire, and
far, far more worldly. She had to grit her teeth to
stop herself from making any comment. It was no
business of hers what Blake did with his life. As
she had already told him she had known they
would have to meet during her stay, but not like
this, in the enforced intimacy of the kitchen of
what had once been their home. Not that she had
ever been allowed to spend much time in here. The
kitchen had been the province of Blake's aunt, a
formidable woman who had made Sapphire feel
awkward and clumsy every time she set foot in it.

'What happened to your aunt?' she questioned
him, trying not to remember all the small
humiliations she had endured here in this room,
but it was too late. They all came flooding back,
like the morning she had insisted on getting up
early to make Blake's breakfast. She had burned
the bacon and broken the eggs while his aunt
stood by in grim silence. Blake had pushed his
plate away with his food only half eaten. She was
barely aware of her faint sigh. The ridiculous thing
had been that she had been and still was quite a
good cook. Her father's housekeeper had taught
her, but being watched by Aunt Sarah had made

her too nervous to concentrate on what she was doing; that and the fact that she had been trying too hard; had been far too eager to please Blake. So much so that in the end her eagerness had been her downfall.

'Nothing. She's living in the South of England with a cousin. I'll tell her you've been enquiring about her next time I write,' Blake mocked, glancing at the heavy watch strapped to his wrist. 'Look I'd better ring your father and tell him you're okay. I'll run you over there in the morning and then see what we can do about your car.'

'No! No, I'd rather go tonight. My father's a sick man Blake,' she told him. 'I'm very anxious to see him.'

'You don't have to tell me how ill he is,' Blake told her explosively, 'I'm the one who told *you*—remember? Don't expect me to believe that you're really concerned about him Sapphire. Not when you haven't been to see him in four years.'

'There were reasons for that.' Her throat was a tight band of pain, past which she managed to whisper her protest.

'Oh yes, like you didn't want to leave your lover?' His lips drew back in a facsimile of a smile, the vulpine grin of a marauding wolf. 'What's the matter Sapphire? Did you hope to keep your little affair a secret?'

'Affair?' Sapphire sat bolt upright in her chair.

'Yes ... with your boss ... the man you're planning to marry, according to your father. What took you so long?'

'It's only five months since I got the divorce,' Sapphire reminded him stiffly.

'But you could have got an annulment—much,

much faster. . . Why didn't you? Or was it that by the time you realised that you could, that the grounds no longer existed?'

It took a physical effort not to get up and face him with the truth, but somehow she managed it.

'My relationship with Alan is no concern of yours Blake,' she told him coolly. 'I'm sorry I've put you to all this trouble, but I'd like to get to Flaws as soon as possible.'

'Meaning you'd like to get away from me as soon as possible,' Blake drawled. 'Well my dear that may not be as easy as you think. In fact I suspect that when I ring your father now and tell him you're here, he'll suggest you stay the night.'

'Stay the night? Here with you, when the farm's only five miles up the road, don't be ridiculous.'

She glared at him, her eyes flashing angrily.

'You know it's probably just as well that you and I have had this opportunity to talk Sapphire. Your father's perked up a lot since you told him you were coming back. He hopes you and I will bury our differences and get back together.'

Stunned, Sapphire could only stare at him. 'You must be mad,' she stammered at last. 'We're divorced . . . my father. . .'

'Your father is a very sick man, still as concerned about the future of his family's land as he was. . .'

'When you married me so that you could inherit it,' Sapphire broke in. 'You took advantage of my naiveté once Blake, but I'm not a seventeen-year-old adolescent in the grips of her first crush now. We're divorced and that's the way we're going to stay.'

'Even if that means precipitating your father's death?'

She went white with the cruelty of his words. 'His death, but. . .'

'Make no mistake about it, your father's a very sick man Sapphire. Very sick indeed, and worse, he's a man with no will left to struggle. You know that he's always wanted to see the two farms united. That was why he wanted us to get married in the first place.'

'If he's so keen for you to have the land, why doesn't he simply give it to you?' Sapphire asked him angrily.

'Because he wants to think some day that a child of ours—carrying his blood as well as mine—will inherit Bell land.'

'Oh so it isn't just marriage you want from me,' Sapphire stormed, 'it's a child as well? I wonder that you dare suggest such a thing when. . .'

'When?' Blake prodded softly when she stopped abruptly. 'When you couldn't bring yourself to touch me when we were married,' she had been about to say, but the pain of that time still hurt too much for her to be able to talk about it.

'When you know that I'm planning to marry someone else,' she told him coolly. 'Blake, I don't believe a word of what you've just said. My father must know that there isn't a chance of you and I getting together again. For one thing, there's simply nothing that such a relationship could offer me.'

'No.' His eyes fell to her breasts, and although Sapphire knew that the bulky wool of her jumper concealed them, she was acutely aware of a peculiar tension invading her body, making her face hot and her muscles ache.

'I would have said that being able to give your father a considerable amount of peace of mind would be a powerful incentive—to most daughters, but then you aren't like most daughters are you Sapphire?' he asked savagely. 'Or like most women for that matter. You don't care who you hurt or how much as long as you get what you want. Look, I don't want to be re-married to you any more than you want it, but I doubt it would be for very long.'

He watched her pale, and sway, with merciless eyes. 'Your father knows already how little time he's got, and whether you want to admit it or not he's very concerned about the future of his land— land which has been in his family as long as this farm has been in mine. Would it hurt either of us so much to do what he wants—to re-marry and stay together until. . .'

'Until he dies?' She hurled the words at him, shaking with pain and anger. 'And for how long do you estimate we should have to play out this charade Blake? You must know, you certainly seem to know everything else.'

'I was the closest thing to family he has left,' Blake told her simply, 'Naturally his doctor . . .' he broke off, studying the quarry tile floor and then raised his head and it seemed to Sapphire that she had been wrong in her original estimation that he hadn't changed. Now he looked older, harder, and she knew with an undeniable intuition that no matter what lies he might tell her about everything else, Blake did genuinely care for her father. Despair welled up inside her. Her father dying. . .

Remorse gripped her insides, her throat tense and sore. She badly wanted to cry, but she couldn't let Blake see her break down.

'Six months or so Sapphire,' he said quietly at last. 'Not a lot to ask you to give up surely? And you have my word that afterwards . . . that we can part quickly and amicably. This time our marriage will be dissolved.'

'And the farm . . . my father's land?'

'I'd like to buy it from you—at the going rate of course, unless your London lover wants to try his hand at farming?'

Just for a moment Sapphire taxed her imagination trying to picture Alan leading Blake's life. Alan would hate it, and she couldn't keep on the farm and work it herself. Even so, all her instincts warned her against agreeing to Blake's suggestion.

'It's a ridiculous idea, Blake,' she told him at last, taking a deep breath.

'You mean you're too selfish to acknowledge its merits,' he countered. 'I thought you might have grown up Sapphire; might have come to realise that there are other things in life apart from the gratification of your own wants, but obviously I was wrong. Come on,' he finished curtly, 'I'll take you 5o Flaws.'

He strode across the kitchen, thrusting open the door without waiting to see if she was following him. Wincing as she got up from the ache in her ankle, Sapphire hobbled to the door. Cold air rushed in to embrace her in its frosty grip. Across the cobbled yard she could make out the bulky shape of the Land-Rover. Blake opened the door and started up the engine. He must be able to see that she was having difficulty walking, Sapphire fumed as she was caught in the beam of the headlights, but he made no effort to help her.

It was only when she reached the Land Rover that he finally got out, walking round to the passenger side to open the door for her. When his hands suddenly gripped her waist she froze, her whole body tensing in rejection, her stiff, 'don't touch me,' making him tense in return. She could feel it in the grip of his fingers, digging through the wool of her jumper to burn into her skin. 'What the hell. . .' For a moment he seemed about to withdraw and then he spun her round, the proximity of his body forcing her back against the cold metal of the Land Rover. 'What is it you're so afraid of Sapphire,' he mocked, his gold eyes searching her too pale face. 'Not me, surely.' His eyes narrowed. 'As I remember it I barely touched you. So it must be yourself.'

'I'm not frightened of anything Blake,' she managed to reply coolly, still holding herself rigid within the grip of his hands. The warmth of his breath lifted her hair, and she was so acutely aware of him that it was a physical agony. Why, oh why had she come back? She had thought herself strong enough to cope, but she wasn't. Blake still had the power to upset and disturb her. He made her feel just as awkward and insecure as he had done when she was seventeen. 'I just don't want you touching me.'

'Frightened I might make you forget all about your London lover?' The soft goading tone of his voice was too much for her. Drawing in her breath on a sharp gasp she said coldly. 'That would be impossible.' She turned away as she spoke, leaning into the Land Rover. Blake's fingers continued to dig into her waist and then he was lifting her, almost throwing her into the seat with a force that jolted the breath from her body and made her aware of her aching bruises.

He didn't speak until he was in the Land-Rover beside her, his eyes fixed on the fog-shrouded lane as he said softly, 'Don't challenge me Sapphire—not unless you want me to accept your challenge. You've come back from London with some fine haughty airs, no doubt meant to keep country bumpkins like myself in their place but it wouldn't take much for me to forget mine Sapphire. There's one hell of a lot of anger inside me towards you, and believe me it would give me great pleasure to give it release.'

Why should Blake be angry? Resentment burned through Sapphire as they drove towards Flaws Farm. She was the one who should be that; and not just angry but bitter too. Blake had never wanted her; he had callously used her adolescent adoration of him, had ruthlessly exploited her feelings, and now he was saying he was angry. He could say what he liked, but there was no way she was going to agree to his outrageous suggestion that they re-marry. Did he think she was totally without intelligence? She knew what he wanted well enough—the same thing he had always wanted. Her father's land. The Seftons and the Bells hadn't always been friendly to one another, and the border reiver had spawned a race of men who all possessed his reckless touch of acquisitiveness. There had been several Seftons who had cast covetous eyes on Flaws farm and thought to make it theirs, but so far none had ever succeeded.

Now she was being foolish, Sapphire chided

herself. Blake was no border reiver, for all that he had inherited his wild ancestors' darkly Celtic looks, and it was true that her father admired and respected him, but surely not to the extent of wanting her, his daughter, to put herself within his power once more?

Sapphire darted a glance at Blake. He was concentrating on his driving, his profile faintly hawkish, his hands assured and knowing as he turned the wheel. There was nothing indecisive or unsure about Blake, she acknowledged. That was what she had admired so much in him as a teenager, and even now, watching him she was conscious of a faint frisson of awareness, a purely feminine acknowledgment of his masculinity. Stop it, she warned herself as they turned into Flaws Farm Lane. Stop thinking about him.

When the Land Rover stopped, she glanced uncomfortably at him. 'Are you coming in with me?'

'Do you really want me to?' he asked mockingly, before shaking his head. 'No, unlike you Sapphire, I'm not hard enough to raise hopes in your father's heart that I can't fulfil. Your father means a lot to me,' he added, startling her with his admission. 'I've always admired him, even patterned myself on him as a youngster I suppose—my own grandfather was too cold and distant—he never ceased mourning my father. I'd give a lot to see your father happy.'

'And even more to make sure that you get Flaws land,' Sapphire threw at him bitterly, 'even to the extent of marrying me. I fell for it once Blake, I'm not going to fall for it again.'

It was only as she struggled across the yard that

she remembered about her luggage, still in Alan's
car. It was too late to turn round and call Blake
back now, he was already reversing out of the
yard. Sighing, Sapphire found the familiar back
door and unlatched it. The kitchen was much as
she remembered it. Her father used to employ a
housekeeper to look after the house, but she had
retired just after Sapphire's marriage. For a while
he had managed with daily help from the village,
but now it seemed he was employing someone else.

The door to the hall opened as Sapphire stepped
into the kitchen and a woman entered the room.
For a second they stared at one another and then
the woman smiled tentatively, offering her hand.
'Mary,' she introduced herself, 'and you must be
Sapphire. Your father's been worrying about you.'

There was just enough reproof in the calm,
softly burred voice for Sapphire to flush and feel
at a disadvantage. Mary was somewhere in her late
thirties, plumpish with smooth brown hair and
warm eyes. The sort of calm, serene, capable
woman she had always envied.

'I'm sorry about that.' Quickly she explained
how she had been delayed, warmed by the quick
sympathy in the hazel eyes.

'May I see my father?' Sapphire asked tentatively. She had been nerving herself for this
moment ever since Blake had told her the
seriousness of her father's condition, and her
palms were damp and sticky as she followed Mary
up the familiar stairs. Her father's bedroom had
windows that looked out over the hills, but tonight
the curtains were drawn to obscure the view.

'It's all right Mary, you can switch the lamp on,'
her father's familiar voice growled as Sapphire

stood awkwardly by the door in the half light. 'I am awake.'

'Sapphire's here,' Mary told him, snapping on the bedside light. Perhaps it was the warm glow from the lamp but her father didn't look as ill as she had anticipated. Her legs felt shaky as she approached his bed, regret, guilt, and a dozen other emotions clamouring for expression. In the end all she could manage was a choked 'Dad,' and then she was in her father's arms, hugging him tightly, trying not to give way to tears.

'Well now, and how's my lass? Let me have a look at you.' As he held her slightly away from him, studying her features, Sapphire studied his. Her father had always had a tall, spare frame, but now he was gaunt, almost painfully thin, the weathered tanned face she remembered frighteningly pale—a sick-room pallor Sapphire acknowledged.

'Dad, if only I'd known. . .'

'Stop tormenting yourself, I wouldn't let Blake tell you. You're far too thin,' he scolded. 'Mary will have to feed you up while you're here. Borders' men don't like their women skinny.'

'But London men do,' Sapphire responded, withdrawing from him a little, sensing danger.

'You're later than we expected.'

'Umm, I had a slight accident.' Quickly she explained.

'You should have stayed overnight with Blake.'

'I'm sure neither Blake or I would have felt comfortable if I had Dad,' she said quietly. 'We're divorced now.'

'More's the pity.' He frowned, the happiness fading from his eyes. 'You should never have left him lass, but then you were so young, and young things take things so seriously.'

If anyone had asked her only days ago if her father had accepted her divorce Sapphire would have had no hesitation in saying 'yes' but now, suddenly, she knew he had not. She looked away from the bed, blinking back tears she wasn't sure were for her father or herself. As she did so she saw Mary glance sympathetically at her.

'I'll run you a bath,' she offered, 'You must be exhausted.'

'Yes, you go along to bed,' her father agreed. 'We'll talk in the morning.' He closed his eyes, his face almost waxen with exhaustion and fear pierced her. Her father was going to die. Until now she hadn't truly accepted it, but suddenly seeing him, seeing his frailty she did. 'Dad, who's looking after the farm?' she asked him trying to force back the painful knowledge.

'Why Blake of course.' He looked surprised that she needed to ask. 'And a fine job he's doing of it too.'

Mary's hand on her arm drew her away from the bed. On the landing Sapphire turned to the older woman, unable to hold back her tears any longer. 'Why?' she asked bitterly. 'Why did no-one tell me? Get in touch with me, I'd no idea. . .'

Shaking her head Mary gestured downstairs, not speaking until Sapphire had followed her down and they were back in the kitchen. 'Blake said not to,' she said quietly, 'he thought it best. At least at first.'

Blake had thought . . . Blake had said. . . Bitterness welled up inside her coupled with a fierce jealousy as she acknowledged something she had always kept hidden even from herself. Her father would have preferred a son ... a male to continue the family line and although he loved her, it was to Blake that he had always confided his innermost thoughts, Blake who he thought of as a son ... Blake who he turned to when he needed someone to lean on and not her.

'There, sit down and cry it all out,' Mary said gently. 'It must have come as a shock to you.'

'Is it true that ... that my father...' Sapphire couldn't go on. Tears were streaming down her face and she dug in her jeans pocket for a handkerchief. 'He's been a very sick man,' Mary said compassionately, her eyes sliding away from Sapphire's. 'His heart isn't too strong and this bout of pneumonia, but having you home has given him a real fillip.'

'I never knew how he felt about the divorce until tonight.' Sapphire almost whispered the words, saying them more to herself than Mary, but the other woman caught them and smiled sympathetically. 'Blake means a lot to him,' she agreed, 'he thought that your marriage protected both you and Flaws land.'

'He worries a lot about the land doesn't he?' Sapphire's voice was unconsciously bitter.

'And about you,' Mary told her. 'The land is like a sacred trust to him and he has a strong sense of duty and responsibility towards it.'

'Strong enough to want to see Blake and me back together again?' Sapphire asked bleakly.

Mary said nothing, but the way her eyes refused to meet Sapphire's told her what she wanted to know.

'You obviously know my father very well,' she

said quietly at last. 'He confides in you far more than he ever confided in me.'

'I'm a trained nurse,' Mary told her, 'and that is how I first came to know your father. When he was first ill he needed a full-time nurse. Dr Forrest recommended me, and your father asked me to stay on as his housekeeper-cum-nurse. The relationship between patient and nurse is one of trust. It has to be. I can't deny that your father, like many people of his generation, doesn't wholly approve of divorce, and he does feel that the land would be properly cared for by Blake, and. . .'

'And that if Blake and I had a son that son would inherit Flaws Farm and would also be half Bell.'

Sapphire signed, suddenly feeling intensely tired. Too much had happened too soon, and she couldn't take it all in.

'There was a 'phone call for you,' Mary added, 'an Alan. I said you'd ring back in the morning.'

Alan! Sapphire started guiltily. She had almost forgotten about him, and even more unforgivably she had forgotten about his car. The BMW was Alan's pride and joy and he wouldn't be too pleased to hear about her accident.

Tomorrow, she thought wearily as she climbed into bed. Tomorrow she would think about what had happened. Somehow she would have to convince her father that there was no chance of her and Blake getting together again. Selfish, Blake had called her. Was she? Her father had very little time left to live . . . six months or so . . . if she re-married Blake she would be giving her father a gift of happiness and peace of mind which surely meant more than her own pride and freedom? She wasn't seventeen any more, held in thrall by her adoration of Blake. She could handle him now as she hadn't been able to do then. A six-month marriage which would be quickly annulled—six months out of her life as payment for her father's peace of mind. What ought she to do?

CHAPTER THREE

'Good morning.' Mary smiled a warm welcome at Sapphire as she walked into the kitchen. 'I was just about to bring you up a cup of tea.'

'Yes, I've overslept disgracefully,' Sapphire said wryly. Time was when she had thought nothing of getting up at half-past five with her father.

'You were exhausted, what with the accident and all. Oh that reminds me, Blake rang. He said not to panic about your luggage. He's bringing it over later when he comes to see your father. He calls in most days,' she added, plugging in the kettle. 'Your father looks forward to his visits, Blake keeps him up to date on how the farm's running.'

'May I go up and see my father?' Sapphire didn't want to think about Blake right now. He had occupied far too many of her thoughts already.

'Of course.' Again Mary smiled warmly. 'Would you like to have your breakfast first?'

'Just a cup of coffee will be fine,' Sapphire assured her. 'I'll go up now.' Before Blake arrives, she could have added, but didn't. Somehow, quite how she didn't know yet, but somehow she was going to have to find a way to explain to her father that she and Blake were parted for good. Even now she could still remember the agony of those first months in London, of having to come to terms with the truth about her marriage; about Blake's feelings for her. He had tolerated her because he wanted the farm. He had never loved her, never desired her and knowing that she had not seen these truths had diminished her self-esteem to such an extent that she had felt somehow as though everyone who saw her or spoke to her, must share Blake's opinion of her. The only way she could escape had been to shut herself off mentally from the rest of the world. There had been days when she felt like dying; days when she would have given anything simply not to wake up in the morning. But all that was past now, she reminded herself. She had overcome the trauma of Blake's rejection; had put the past and all that it held, safely behind her. But she couldn't forget it, she acknowledged. She still occasionally had those terrible dreams when she was forced to witness Blake making love to Miranda, when she had to endure the sound of their mocking laughter. How she had hated herself; *everything* about herself, from her height to the colour of her hair, torturing herself by imagining how many times Blake must have looked at her and put Miranda in her place. The only thing that surprised her was that Blake hadn't married. Those love letters she had found had obviously been meant for Miranda.

No-one, not even Alan knew how totally Blake had rejected her; physically, mentally and emotionally. And facing up to that knowledge had driven her almost to the point where she lost her sanity. But she had emerged from it all a stronger person. Being forced to come face to face with the truth had made her re-evaluate herself completely. No man would ever hurt her now as Blake had done. She allowed no-one to come close enough to her to do so.

If Alan did propose to her she would probably accept him. She wanted a family; she and Alan got on well. She would never feel for him what she had once felt for Blake, but then he would never look at her body, imagining it was another woman's, he would never lie to her, or look at her with contempt. Blake was an arrogant bastard, she thought bitterly as she stood at the top of the stairs, poised to enter her father's room. After what he'd done to her, she didn't know how he had the nerve to suggest what he had.

'Sapphire.' Her father greeted her happily, from his chair by the window. The cold March sunshine picked out with cruel clarity the signs of wasting on his face, and Sapphire was overwhelmed with a rush of emotion.

'Dad.' She went over to him, hugging him briefly and then turning away before he could see her tears.

'What's this?' Her eye was caught by the heavy, leather bound book on his lap. 'Don't tell me you're actually reading something, other than a farming magazine,' she teased. Never once during her childhood could she remember seeing her father reading. He had always been an active, physical man more at home in his fields than in the house. It saddened her unbearably to see him like this. Why . . . why? she cried bitterly inside.

'It's the family Bible.' His smile was as she had always remembered it. 'I haven't looked at it since your mother wrote your name inside.'

After her, her mother had not been able to have any more children. Had she too, like Sapphire, sensed how much her father felt the lack of a male heir? Had that in part contributed to the break-up of their marriage? Questions she would never know the answer to now, Sapphire thought dully, watching her father open the Bible.

His hand trembled slightly as he touched the old paper. 'This Bible goes back as far as 1823, and it lists the birth of every Bell since.' He gave a faint sigh and closed it. 'I had hoped I might see the name of your's and Blake's child added to that list, but now. . .' He turned away dejectedly.

The words Sapphire had intended to say died unspoken. A tight knot of pain closed her throat. She reached out her hand touching her father's shoulder, 'Dad. . .' He turned to look at her, and as though the words were coming from another person, she heard herself saying shakily, 'Blake and I are going to try again. I . . . we . . . we talked about it last night.' She looked out of the window without seeing the view. Could her father honestly believe that what she was saying was true? Perhaps not, but he would accept it *as* the truth because he wanted to believe it was so desperately; just as she had once desperately wanted to believe that Blake loved her.

'You mean the two of you plan to re-marry?'

'We may. . .' What on earth had she got herself into? Panic clawed at her. She *couldn't* marry Blake again. But she had just told her father that she might.

'I suppose if we do it will make the local tongues wag.'

'Not necessarily. I don't think Blake's ever told anyone that you're divorced. Most people think you're still just separated.'

Why hadn't Blake told them? Could it be that he was using her father's illness as a lever to force her

to fall in with his plans? He would buy the land
from her, he had told her, but as her husband he
wouldn't need to buy it, and being married to her
need not stop him from finding love elsewhere. It
hadn't stopped him before.

She *must* tell her father that she had changed her
mind, she thought frantically, she must tell him
now, before this thing went any further. Even now
she couldn't believe that he was dying. He looked
ill yes, but... But hadn't she learned the futility
of self-deception yet?

'Dad. . .'

'Isn't that the Land Rover?' he asked interrupt-
ing her. 'Blake must have arrived.'

'Dad, I. . .'

Both of them turned at the sound of firm
footsteps on the stairs, Sapphire unconsciously
blending into the shadows of the room as the door
was thrust open and Blake strode in. Strangely his
eyes met hers almost immediately, as though he
had known by instinct where she was.

'Blake, Sapphire's just told me the good news.'
If she hadn't known better she might almost have
believed the look the two men exchanged was one
of complicity, but even as the thought formed it
was gone as her father turned his head and the
harsh light through the window made her acutely
conscious of his illness.

'Has she now.' For a man who spent so much of
his live outdoors Blake moved exceptionally
gracefully, and far too swiftly. She had no
opportunity to avoid him as he walked towards
her, lean brown fingers curling round her upper
arm. 'And do you approve?'

'Need you ask?'

'Not really.'

'I'm sure you two have lots to discuss.' Sapphire snapped out the words bitterly, resenting their male unanimity. 'I must go and telephone Alan. He doesn't know about his car yet.'

'Or about us,' Blake reminded her, and while the look in his eyes might have been mistaken for one of possessive hunger Sapphire knew it was for her father's land rather than for her.

Outside the room she paused on the landing feeling acutely sick. Why had she said what she had to her father? Heaven only knew, she didn't want to be married to Blake again, no matter how temporarily. And yet her father had been pleased; pleased and relieved and surely for six months. . . Gnawing on her bottom lip she walked down to the kitchen and picked up the 'phone. Alan answered almost straight away.

'Where've you been?' he demanded. 'I expected you to ring hours ago.'

'I overslept I'm afraid. Alan, I had an accident last night and damaged your car.' She waited for his anxious spate of questions to finish before explaining what had happened. 'Don't let them touch the car—these country garages, God alone knows what sort of damage they might do. I'll come up and sort it out myself.'

'Alan no . . .' Sapphire started to say, but it was too late. 'Look I've got to go,' he told her before she could continue. 'I've got an appointment. I'll be up as soon as I can—possibly in three or four days.'

'Everything okay?' Mary nodded to the kettle. 'Fancy a drink? I normally take one up to your dad about now.'

'No ... no thanks, I think I'll go out for a walk.'

'Well, don't go too far,' Mary cautioned her. 'The temperature's dropping and we might well have snow. Snow in March isn't uncommon up here,' she reminded Sapphire dryly when she raised her eyebrows. 'Many a farmer's lost a crop of newborn lambs to the weather. *You* should know that.'

She needed time to think, Sapphire acknowledged as she walked into the cobbled yard and through into the field beyond; time to come to terms with what she herself had set in motion. She couldn't back out now; that much was plain. How could she have been so stupid as to allow Blake to manoeuvre her into this situation?

But it hadn't been Blake's logical, reasoned arguments that had won her over, it had been her father's pain. Guilt was a terrible burden to carry. She shivered suddenly, conscious that her jumper was no real protection against the bitter east wind, but she wasn't ready to go back to the farm yet. Going back meant facing Blake; and that was something she wasn't ready for yet. But she couldn't avoid him forever, and it was getting colder. Reluctantly she turned and re-traced her steps but when the farm came in sight and she saw that the Land Rover was still there, instead of heading for the house she walked towards the large attached barn.

In the days when Flaws Farm had possessed a small dairy herd this barn had housed them but now it was empty apart from the farmyard hens whose eggs were purely for domestic use. She had kept her pony, Baron, in here and had spent many hours grooming him, preparing him for local agricultural shows. They had even won a couple of prizes. Sighing faintly she wandered deeper into the barn stopping beside the ladder into the hayloft. As a teenager she had retreated up there to read and daydream. The sound of familiar footsteps made her body tense. Even without turning round to look she knew who it was.

'Something told me you might be in here.' Blake's voice was mocking. 'You always did use it as a bolt-hole.'

She turned round, trying to blank all emotion out of her features, while Blake studied her with a slow, insolent appraisal that set her teeth on edge. Inwardly shaking with nerves she refused to let him see how much his presence disturbed her. 'Finished?' she asked sourly. 'What exactly were you doing Blake?'

'Just wondering why you choose to wear such masculine clothes.' It was a blatantly challenging statement when coupled with his open study of her, and to her resentment she knew she had already been betrayed into a response to it, even if it was only in the increased stiffening of her muscles.

'These happen to be the only clothes I had this morning. No doubt you like your women dulcet and feminine, compliant and obedient, but I'm not like that Blake. Not any more.'

'No, you're not are you?' There was just a suspicion of laughter trailing in his voice, enough to make her stare back at him aggressively and refuse to give way as he came towards her. 'I also like them aroused and responsive—just as you are at the moment.'

The explosive denial trembling on her lips died as he reached forward, his thumb stroking along her throat to rest on the point where her pulse thudded betrayingly. 'Anger is a form of arousal isn't it?' he mocked lightly. 'And you *are* angry with me, aren't you Sapphire?'

'Not as much as I am with myself,' she told him curtly, drawing away. She wasn't going to give Blake any advantages this time. 'What I said to you last night still holds good, I don't want to marry you.'

'But you told your father that you did.'

'No. I told him that I *was* doing. I didn't mean to, but before I could retract you arrived.'

'And now?' He asked the question softly, watching her with eyes that gave nothing of his own feelings away.

'I'll have to go through with it—you know that. You saw how he reacted. Dear God, even now I can't believe that I'm going to lose him.' She paced distractedly, too strung up to give way to tears and yet needing to release some of her nervous energy.

'And what about the boyfriend—have you told *him*?'

'Alan? No . . . not yet, but he's coming up for his car soon, I'll tell him then.'

'How soon is soon?' Blake asked idly. 'Because in three days' time we'll be married.'

Three days! She looked up at him, not even attempting to hide her shock. 'So soon?'

Blake shrugged his shoulders and against her will Sapphire found herself comparing the masculine breadth of them to Alan's. Even dressed in faded jeans· and an old woollen checked shirt Blake possessed a lithe masculine sensuality that

Alan would never have, for all his expensive tailoring Alan believed that appearances were important and Sapphire wouldn't have denied it, but Blake was one of those men who could afford to break life's rules. Angrily she pushed the thought away.

'Why wait?' Blake asked laconically. 'The sooner it's done the happier your father will be.'

'He told me that most people up here don't even know that we're divorced.' Her voice gave away her anger.

'Most people? No-one knows,' Blake corrected, blandly.

'Not even Miranda?'

His eyebrows rose, and Sapphire felt her face flush. What on earth had possessed her to bring Miranda's name up? She had no interest in Blake's love life—it was his own affair.

'Why mention Miranda in particular?' Blake mocked.

'Perhaps because it's the sort of thing a man would tell his mistress,' Sapphire came back curtly. 'After all you told her that our marriage . . . wasn't consummated.'

'How do you know that?' His voice had sharpened, hardened almost, but he had turned slightly away so that Sapphire couldn't see his expression, but she had definitely caught him off guard. Good, she thought, watching him. Obviously he didn't know what Miranda had said to her.

'Because she told me.' She shrugged disdainfully as he turned round and stared at her with cold hard, golden eyes. 'It was at the same time as she told me about the weekend the two of you spent in the Cotswolds actually.' Giving him a cold smile she marched past, heading for the barn door. It would do him good to realise that she wasn't as naive as he had always believed, but just as she drew level with the door his arm snaked out, his fingers curling painfully round her wrist.

'And that, of course, was why you left me?'

'It was *one* of the reasons—there were others.' It was her turn to shrug dismissively. 'But none of that matters now, I merely asked about Miranda so that I could be prepared for any situation that might arise.'

'She doesn't know we're divorced,' Blake told her. 'After my experiences with you I decided I preferred the life of a bachelor.'

'And having a wife tucked away in the background made it all a lot simpler. Yes I can see that. Let me go Blake, I want to go back to the house.'

'Isn't there something you've forgotten?'

She frowned, glancing uncertainly at him.

'Loving partners normally part with a kiss,' he told her mockingly.

'Maybe *they* do, but there's nothing "loving" about our relationship,' Sapphire snapped. 'You didn't want to kiss me four years ago Blake, I can hardly see why you would want to now.'

'No? Perhaps I want to see how much your London lover has taught you.' His head bent towards her and Sapphire immediately tensed trying to pull away, but Blake was still gripping her wrist. His free arm fastened round her, his hand on the small of her back forcing her against him.

A mixture of sensations raced through her as the

heat of his body imposed itself against her; anger; tension, but most of all a resurgence of a familiar vulnerability she thought she had long ago overcome. The knowledge that she hadn't, blinded her to everything else. She trembled against Blake, closing her eyes to blot out his mocking smile trying to convince herself that she was wrong; that the panic storming through her came from anger and not from fear.

But what was it she feared? Not Blake. No, herself, she admitted sensing the downward descent of his mouth, and twisting away to avoid it. Not Blake, but herself, her vulnerability towards him; her. . .

His mouth brushed hers and she tensed. 'Is that *all* you've learned? Not very good,' Blake drawled, as his mouth moved from her lips to her ear. His tongue tip explored the delicate shaping of her ear and panic exploded inside her. She mustn't let him do this to her, she. . . Another moment and he would be kissing her again and this time. . . No she wouldn't let him see that he could evoke a response from her . . . a response that was really surely nothing more than a conditioned echo of the old feeling she had had for him?

His mouth was feathering across her skin towards her lips. Taking her courage in both hands, Sapphire turned to meet it, willing herself to relax. She had dated several men in London before settling for Alan, and surely she had learned enough technique from them to show Blake that she wasn't a frightened seventeen-year-old any more.

Forcing herself to ignore the screaming protest of her nerves Sapphire opened her mouth inviting his deeper invasion, teasing him with the tip of her tongue. She actually felt the sudden tension in his muscles, the quickly controlled start of surprise, but her brief advantage was lost as Blake's arms tightened around her, his mouth taking what she had so recklessly offered, his lips harshly possessive against hers.

If only he had kissed her like this when she was seventeen. The thought surfaced through a whirling jet-stream of jumbled emotions, fiercely clamped down as soon as she acknowledged it, and pushed Blake away.

He let her go, watching her with unblinking gold eyes. Almost as though he willed her to do it, Sapphire ran her tongue over the swollen contours of her mouth. 'Well, well... That was quite something.'

His mouth was wry where she had expected it to be triumphant, because she couldn't deny to herself that there had been a moment in his arms when she had forgotten everything that lay between them and she had responded to him in a way she had never responded to any other man, but if anything he looked angry.

'He's obviously taught you well.' The comment bordered on the harshly accusatory and coming from anyone else Sapphire would have instantly taken exception to it, but sensing that for some reason she had got under his skin she responded lightly. 'And very extensively, I'm not seventeen any more Blake.'

'No, you're not are you,' he agreed, 'so don't expect me to handle you with kid gloves will you?'

'I don't expect you to "handle" me at all Blake—that's part of our agreement—remember?'

'Oh I think I'll be able to, now, but will you?'

He turned on his heel and left before she could speak, and although Sapphire told herself it was relief that made her shake so much that she had to lean against the stairs, in reality she knew that her emotions were far more complex than that.

What had she let herself in for agreeing to re-marry Blake? She had always known he must despise her, but the anger she had just seen, so savage and bitter, that was something she hadn't guessed at. He must want Flaws Farm very badly, she thought bleakly as she made her way on shaky legs back to the house.

'Blake gone?' her father asked, when she walked into his room. Already he looked much better, and Sapphire realised with an aching pang how much her marriage to Blake meant to him.

'Yes.' She couldn't inject any enthusiasm into her voice. 'Never mind.' Her father obviously mistook the reason for her listlessness. 'You'll be seeing him tonight. He's taking you out to celebrate—at least that's what he said to me.'

To celebrate! Sapphire grimaced, inwardly resenting the fact that Blake hadn't said anything to her about going out. Had he done so, she would have refused.

'I can't tell you how much it means to me that the pair of you are getting back together again,' her father said quietly. 'He's a fine man Sapphire. A good strong man, the sort of man you need.'

She made her escape from the room without giving any response, half-blinded by the weak tears threatening to obscure her vision. In her own room she opened the suitcase Blake must have brought up. Even to think of him walking into her room made prickles of antagonism run down her spine. How on earth was she going to live with him for six months when she hated him so much?

She hadn't brought much with her, certainly nothing she could go out in to 'celebrate'—and nothing she could wear to get married in. Fresh tears blurred her eyes as she remembered the dress she had worn the first time they were married. Stupid sentimentality, she derided herself; their wedding had just been another part of Blake's elaborate charade, just like the half-reverent, almost worshipping kiss he had given her just outside the church doors. Sighing, Sapphire hung up her clothes. She would wear the plain black wool dress she had brought; it was a perfect foil for her colouring and a perfect accompaniment for her mood; Alan had always liked her in it.

Alan! She hadn't told him yet about Blake. She gnawed on her lip uncertain as to whether to ring him, or wait until he came up. She was sure he would understand; Alan was always logical and reasonable. For the first time it struck her just what she had committed herself to. She would have to give up her job; her flat; her London life; everything she had fought so hard for when she left Blake. But surely it was a small price to pay for her father's peace of mind? But say Alan did not accept her decision. She would not only have lost her job, she would have lost a good friend and potential lover as well. She couldn't understand why the knowledge should cause her so little pain. Perhaps the agony of meeting Blake again; of being forced to remember how much he had hurt her had anaesthetised her against other, lesser hurts. Sighing she finished unpacking and went downstairs. One thing she did remember about farm life was that there was always work to be done and work, as she had learned in London, was a very effective panacea.

'I'm just going down to the village to do some shopping and pick up your father's prescription,' Mary told her when Sapphire asked if there was anything she could do. 'Want to come with me?'

'No, I'll stay here if you don't mind.' Sapphire frowned. 'I would have thought the doctor would call every day, in view of Dad's illness.'

Mary eyed her sympathetically. 'There's really no point now,' she said gently. 'Are you sure you won't come with me?'

'No . . . no thanks.'

'Well I'll be on my way then. I want to call at the butchers, your father loves shepherd's pie and I thought I'd make one for him tonight.'

How could Mary be so matter of fact, Sapphire wondered, watching the other woman driving away, but then as a nurse she would be used to death; she would have learned to accept the inevitable. As *she* had not, Sapphire acknowledged, but then she had had so little time to come to terms with the reality of her father's condition. Blake had broken the news to her almost brutally. The way he did everything. Unable to settle to anything she went up to her father's room, but he was asleep. Not wanting to disturb his rest she left again. What on earth could she do with herself? Perhaps she ought to have gone with Mary. She wandered aimlessly into the yard, bending to pet the sheepdog that suddenly emerged from the field. Tam, the shepherd followed close behind, a smile splitting his weather-seamed face as he recognised her. Tam had been her father's shepherd for as long as she could remember. He had seemed old to her when she was a child, and she wondered how old he was. He was one of a dying breed; a man who preferred the solitude of the hills, spending most of the summer in his small cottage watching over his flocks. The rich acres of farmland in the valley were given over to crops now, but her father still maintained his flock of sheep on his hill pastures.

'Weather's going to turn bad,' Tam told her laconically, 'Ought to get the sheep down off the hills, especially the ewes. Suppose I'd better get over to Sefton and see Blake,' he added morosely, whistling to his dog.

Watching them go Sapphire realised the extent of Blake's influence on Flaws Farm. No wonder he didn't want to lose the land. He probably looked on it as his own already. She had wanted to protest to Tam that her father was the one to ask about the sheep, but instinctively she had known that Tam wouldn't have understood. What she considered to be Blake's interference would be taken as good neighbourliness by the old shepherd.

As she walked back into the kitchen the 'phone was ringing, and she answered it automatically.

'Sapphire, is that you?'

'Yes, Blake.'

'I forgot to mention it this morning, but I'll be round about seven-thirty tonight to take you out to dinner, and before you say anything, I didn't plan it. It was your father who mentioned it; he seemed to think some sort of celebration was in order, and I think he's probably right. If we're seen dining together, it won't come as too much of a surprise to people when they know we're back together.'

'Surprise? Don't you mean shock?' Sapphire gritted into the receiver. 'Especially where your female friends are concerned Blake.'

'If I didn't know better I might almost believe that you're jealous.'

'Funny,' Sapphire snapped back. 'I never realised you had such a powerful imagination. I must go now Blake,' she lied, 'Dad's calling me.'

'See you tonight.'

She hung up quickly leaving her staring at the black receiver. How could her life have changed so radically and so fast. One moment she had been looking forward to her holiday with Alan; to their relationship perhaps deepening from friendship into marriage, convinced that she had laid the ghosts in her past, and now, so swiftly that she could scarcely comprehend even now how it had happened, her life had somehow become entangled with Blake's again, but this time she was older and wiser. She had been burned once—so badly that there was no way she was ever going to approach the fire again.

But fire has a way of luring its victims, she acknowledged, bitterly, just like love.

CHAPTER FOUR

SHE was ready when Blake arrived. He gave her black-clad body a cursory examination as he stepped into the kitchen and then drawled, 'Mourning, Sapphire?'

'It was the only dress I had with me.'

Again those golden eyes studied her body, but this time there was no mocking warmth to light their amber depths as Blake said coolly, 'You should have told me, I've still got a wardrobe-full of your things up at the house, and by the looks of you you could still get into them.'

He made it sound more of an insult than a compliment, and Sapphire turned away so that he wouldn't see the quick flush of colour warming her skin. Why was it that Blake seemed to possess this ability to put her in the wrong, even when she wasn't?

'If you're ready I think we'd better be on our way. I've booked our table for eight.' He glanced at his watch, the brief glimpse she had of his dark sinewy wrist doing strange things to Sapphire's stomach. She recognised the sensation immediately, and it gave her a sickening jolt. She had thought she was long past the stage of experiencing sexual appreciation of something as mundane as a male arm. As a teenager, the merest glimpse of Blake in the distance had been enough to start her stomach churning with excitement but that was all behind her now. Shrugging aside her feelings as an echo of the past she picked up her coat and followed Blake to the door.

To her surprise he hadn't brought the Land Rover but was driving a sleek black BMW. Some of her surprise must have communicated itself to Blake because he glanced at her sardonically, his eyebrows raised as he waited for her to join him, opening the door for her as she reached the car. But then he always had had that air of masculine sophistication, a rare commodity in the Borders where most of the boys she had grown up with thought only of their land and their stock. But she had lived in London for long enough not to be overawed by Blake any longer, surely? Alan was always meticulous about handing her into his car, but his fingers beneath her elbow didn't provoke the same jolting, lightning bolt of sensation that Blake's did, her senses told her treacherously.

Ridiculous to feel so affected by such casual contact—no doubt she was over-reacting. She had had to guard herself against thinking about Blake for so long that she was almost hyper-sensitive to him. Yes, that must be the explanation Sapphire decided as Blake set the car in motion. Of course she was wound-up and tense, who wouldn't be after learning that their father was close to death and that the one thing he wanted in life was the one thing she least desired. Marriage to Blake! She glanced covertly at his profile. He was concentrating on the road, his lips set in a hard line. Reaction suddenly shivered through her. What had she committed herself to? Despite the warmth from the car's heaters she felt chilled, and yet her face seemed to be burning. She *couldn't* go through with it. Her father would understand. She must talk to Blake, she. . .

'If you're having second thoughts, forget them, I'm not letting you back out now Sapphire.' The coldly harsh words cut through her anguished thoughts like a whiplash. How had he known what she was thinking? He was right about one thing though, it was too late to back out now. Her father wanted their reconciliation too desperately.

'Where are we going?' She asked the question more to dispel the tense atmosphere inside the car than because she really wanted to know.

'Haroldgate,' Blake told her briefly.

She only just managed to catch back her protest. Haroldgate was a small village nestling in one of the valleys and as far as she knew it possessed only one restaurant. Blake had taken her there the evening he had proposed to her. She had been so thrilled by his invitation. 'The Barn' at Haroldgate was the most sophisticated eating place in the area and she had never been before. She could vividly recall how impressed she had been by her surroundings, and how tense. Shaking herself mentally she tried to appear unconcerned. 'The Barn' might have seemed the very zenith of sophistication to an awkward seventeen-year-old who had never been anywhere, but it could hardly compare with some of the restaurants Alan had taken her to. Alan was something of a gourmet and discovering new eating places was one of his hobbies. He also liked to be seen in the right places, unlike Blake who had little concern for appearances or being seen to do the 'right thing', Sapphire acknowledged. Neither did Blake make a sacred ritual out of eating as Alan did. Frowning

Sapphire tried to dispel the vague feeling that somehow she was being disloyal to Alan by comparing him with Blake. They were two completely different men who could not be compared, and of the two. . .

'We're here.'

The curt comment broke across her thoughts. Blake stopped the car and in the darkness Sapphire felt him studying her. Her muscles tensed automatically and defensively, although she couldn't have said why.

'I won't have you thinking about him while you're with me,' he told her tersely. 'I won't have it Sapphire, do you understand?'

She was far too taken aback by the tone of his voice to make any immediate comment. How had Blake known she was thinking about Alan? And why should he object? His attitude fanned the embers of resentment that had been burning in her all day.

'You don't own my thoughts Blake,' she told him mockingly, 'and if I choose to think about the man I love that's my affair. You can't stop me.'

'You think not?'

The headlights from another car turning into the carpark illuminated the interior of the BMW briefly and Sapphire was struck by the white tension of Blake's face. Did getting her father's land mean so very much to him? Fear feathered lightly along her spine.

'Don't push me too hard Sapphire,' he warned, as he unfastened his seat belt. 'I *am* only human.'

'You could have fooled me.' She muttered the words flippantly beneath her breath, but he caught them, leaning across to grasp her forearms while she was still fastened into her seat.

'Could I? Then perhaps this will convince you just how human I can be, and not to rely too heavily on your own judgment.' The words carried a thread of bitterness Sapphire couldn't decipher but there was nothing cryptic about the pressure of Blake's mouth against her own, hard and determined as his hands pressed her back into her seat.

It was a kiss of anger and bitterness, even she could recognise that, and yet it called out to something deep inside her; some shadowing of pain she hadn't known still existed and which suddenly became a fierce ache, leaping to meet and respond to the anger she could feel inside Blake.

The result was a devastation of her senses; a complete reversal of everything she had ever thought about herself and her own sexuality; her physical response to Blake so intense and overwhelming that it succeeded in blocking everything else out.

Without her being aware of how it had happened her arms were round his neck, her fingers stroking the thick softness of his hair, and yet it was pain she wanted him to feel—not pleasure, and it was anger she wanted to show him as she returned the fierce intensity of his kiss, and not love.

'You want me.' It was Blake's thick utterance of the words that brought her back to reality. That, and her own bitter mental acknowledgment that somehow he had aroused her, had touched a deep core of need inside her that none of Alan's gentle caresses had ever revealed.

'I *want* Alan,' she lied curtly, 'but since he's not here. . .'

Blake withdrew from her immediately as she had known he would. His pride would never allow him to be a substitute for someone else, but what did surprise Sapphire was that he believed her. But then he could not, as she could, compare her reaction to him with her reaction to Alan. She did love Alan. What she had just experienced in Blake's arms; that bitter tension that had made her body ache and her eyes sting with suppressed tears was just something left over from the past, that was all.

'Are we going to eat, or do you want to spend the rest of the evening in the car?'

The harsh words rasped over too-sensitive nerves. Sapphire pushed Blake's hand away as he reached out to help her with her seat belt, and knew by the tension in his body that she had annoyed him. How on earth were they supposed to live together, supposedly as man and wife, preserving the fiction that they had been reconciled when they reacted so explosively to one another? If only she hadn't made that stupid comment to her father, but he had looked so ill . . . and he had been so pleased, almost as though she had given him a reason to go on fighting to live. And so she had.

The restaurant was just as attractive as she remembered. The old barn had been sensitively restored, and while the atmosphere was not one of luxurious glamour there was something about it that Sapphire found more appealing than any of Alan's favourite haunts.

The Head Waiter recognised Blake immediately and they were swiftly shown to a table for two.

The restaurant wasn't a large one, the proprietors preferring not to expand and risk losing their excellent reputation. As they studied their menus, Sapphire glanced covertly round the room, wondering if she would recognise any of their fellow diners. A couple sat at one table talking and Sapphire stiffened as she recognised Miranda.

Four years ago this woman had been her husband's mistress, and she was still as beautiful as ever Sapphire recognised, and still obviously bemusing the opposite sex if her table companion's expression was anything to go by. Just as Sapphire was about to look away, she raised her head, her eyes narrowing as they met Sapphire's. Conscious that she was staring Sapphire tried to look away and found that she could not. A familiar nausea started to well up inside her, and she fought it down. She was over all that now. She wasn't going to let it happen again, and yet against her will her mind kept on relaying to her mental images of Blake and Miranda together, of Blake's long-legged, narrow-hipped body making love to Miranda's, in all the ways it had never made love to hers. The menu dropped from her fingers as she tried to stem the flood of images. She was over this; she had been over it for years... She knew now that most of her anguish sprang not from the fact that Blake and Miranda had been lovers, but rather from the knowledge that he had desired Miranda as intensely as he had not desired her. If Blake had made love to her she would not have suffered this torment; she and Miranda would have met as equals; as women, not as adult and child.

'Sapphire?'

She realised that Blake was talking to her; watching her, and her face closed up. How much had she already given away? She glanced desperately at him but he was looking at Miranda.

Sapphire followed his look, tensing as she saw the other couple stand up and head towards them.

'Blake.' Miranda's companion held out his hand to Blake, who rose to shake it, but it was at Sapphire that he looked.

'Sapphire.' Miranda's greeting to her was coolly mocking. 'You've barely changed.'

The words were designed to hurt, but Sapphire chose to turn the barb back on its sender. 'In four years?' she murmured, 'How flattering. I must confess I barely recognised you.'

A blatant lie, but she could always use it to explain away her too lengthy scrutiny of the other woman. And she *had* aged, Sapphire noted now. Although she was still very beautiful, she was now more obviously a woman well into her thirties. She must be a year or two older than Blake. Her companion was in his forties, and although he looked pleasant enough, physically he could not compare with Blake.

'Sapphire, let me introduce you to Miranda's husband.' Blake's words were a shock. Her husband? Her eyes went automatically to Miranda's ring hand where a huge diamond solitaire nestled against an obviously new wedding ring.

'Jim is the Senior Registrar at Hexham General.' Blake told her. 'He and Miranda got married a couple of months ago.'

'What brings you back up here Sapphire?' Miranda questioned her.

She started to reply but Blake beat her to it, drawing her hand through his arm, pulling her into the warmth of his side as he said calmly, 'We've decided to give our marriage another try.'

'A rather sudden decision surely?' Icy blue eyes swept over Sapphire, Miranda's tone intimating disbelief.

'Not really.' Blake's voice was as smooth as silk and for the first time, Sapphire was grateful for his ability to conceal the truth. 'It's been on the cards for some time. Sapphire just took a bit of convincing that's all.' His possessive smile was meant to indicate that he considered himself lucky to get her back, but Sapphire wasn't deceived for one moment. There was a subtle tension between Blake and Miranda which suggested to Sapphire that getting her father's land wasn't the sole reason Blake wanted a 'reconciliation'. Had Miranda married to spite Blake? To prove to him that if he didn't want marriage then other men did, and was he now retaliating by announcing their reconciliation? Even worse, had he known that Miranda and Jim would be here tonight?

'Well congratulations to you both.' Jim smiled warmly at them, and took Miranda's arm.

'Yes indeed, better luck this time.' The words were innocuous enough but Sapphire wasn't deceived. She read the venom behind them, and knew that Blake had too.

When the other couple had gone she sat down and picked up her menu. Eating was the last thing she felt like but she was determined not to let Blake see how much seeing Miranda again had disturbed her.

'I'm sorry about that.' His terse apology

stunned her and Sapphire looked up at him. There were deep grooves of tension running from his nose to his mouth. 'I didn't know they'd be here.'

Sapphire shrugged dismissively, 'It doesn't matter. I didn't realise Miranda was married.'

'Why should you?' Blake was curt and abrupt, 'I didn't realise that. . .' He broke off, his mouth grim. 'Look I don't think coming out tonight was such a good idea. Let's leave shall we? I don't think either of us is in the mood for the type of celebration your father had in mind.'

'But what about Miranda?' Sapphire objected. 'If we leave now, she'll never believe what you said about us being reconciled.'

Blake shrugged, standing up to come round and hold her chair as she got to her feet. 'Does it matter what she thinks?' He sounded tense. 'As a matter of fact, what she probably will think is that we've decided we'd rather be making love than eating.'

'Because that's what you'd be doing if you were with her?' The words were out before Sapphire could stop them. 'Aren't you forgetting something,' she added bitterly. 'Miranda knows exactly how undesirable you find me. You told her—remember?'

'I told her nothing,' Blake grated back. 'She tricked that admission out of you, but if it worries you so much I can take you back to Sefton House right now and make you my wife in every sense of the word.'

'Thanks, but no thanks.' Somehow she managed to inject just the right amount of scathing indifference into her voice, but it was hard not to react to his words; not to shiver beneath the rough velvet urgency of his voice, nor to turn to him in blind acceptance of the pleasure it promised, but instead to simply precede him and walk out of the restaurant as calmly as though she were completely unaffected by his words.

Were he and Miranda still lovers? Somehow Sapphire didn't think so; there hadn't been the complicity between them she would have expected had they been. Instead there had been something almost approaching antagonism.

They drove back along the road they had come in a silence which remained unbroken until Sapphire realised that Blake had taken the turning for his own house instead of carrying on to her father's farm.

'Don't worry, I'm not kidnapping you,' he told her sardonically as she turned to him in protest. 'It's barely ten o'clock. If I take you home now your father will think there's something wrong.'

'And he'd be right.' Sapphire muttered the words under her breath but Blake heard them.

'This isn't easy for me either you know,' he told her grittily, 'but why should I expect you to realise that? You were never any good at seeing the other person's point of view.'

'Meaning what exactly?' The anger that had been burning inside her all evening burst into destructive flames. 'That I should have played the "understanding" wife and turned a blind eye to your affair?'

Light spilled out into the cobbled courtyard as Blake pulled up outside his house. He stopped the engine and Sapphire saw him tense almost as though he were bracing himself to do something.

'Sapphire, look, my "affair" as you call it
never...'

'I don't want to hear about it.' She cut across
him quickly. She didn't want to exhume the past;
it was far too painful. Talking about his
relationship with Miranda forced her to remember how intensely she had once longed to
have those brown hands touching her body,
exploring its contours, giving her the pleasure
her feverishly infatuated senses had told her she
could find in his arms. 'It's over Blake,' she
reminded him determinedly. 'We're two different
people now.'

'If you say so.' He unfastened his seat belt and
opened his door. 'Hungry?'

Sapphire shook her head.

'Come inside and have a cup of coffee then, I've
got a mare waiting to foal in the barn, I'll check
up on her and then I'll take you home.'

He didn't invite her to go with him, and
Sapphire stood forlornly in the immaculate
kitchen of Sefton House listening to the sound of
his footsteps dying away as he crossed the yard
and entered the large barn.

Once she had been part of this world, and he
would have thought nothing of inviting her to join
him. Together they had shared the miracle of birth
on many occasions in the past, but now she was
deliberately being excluded. It baffled Sapphire
that the anger she sensed churning inside him
should be directed against her. Blake had no
rational reason for being angry with her: had
someone asked her she would have said he was
incapable of feeling any emotional response
towards her whatsoever.

More to keep herself occupied than because she wanted any she started to make some coffee. The kitchen was immaculate, but somehow impersonal. Presumably he had his own reasons for not replacing his aunt with a housekeeper. At least that was one complication she wouldn't have to face this time. Sarah Sefton had never made any secret of the fact that she considered her far too young for Blake. She had disapproved of her right from the very start, Sapphire mused, watching the aromatic dark-brown liquid filter down into the jug, and breathing in the heavenly smell.

'That smells good.' She hadn't heard Blake return, and she swung round tensely, trying to mask her automatic reaction to him by asking after the mare.

'She's fine. This will be her third foal, and we don't anticipate any problems, but like any other female she needs the reassurance of knowing someone cares.'

He said the words carelessly but the look in his eyes was far from casual as he added softly, 'Does Alan let you know he cares Sapphire?'

'All the time.' She managed a cool smile, 'I've made us some coffee, I hope your "help" won't mind my rummaging in her cupboards.'

'I'm sure she won't,' Blake responded equally blandly, 'but when my aunt retired I decided I preferred having the place to myself. A woman comes up from the village to clean; apart from that I'm self-sufficient.' He saw the assessing glance Sapphire slid over the immaculate kitchen, and said softly, 'I don't spend enough time here to make it untidy. In fact recently I've been eating as many meals at Flaws as I have here.'

'Yes, I haven't thanked you yet for taking on the responsibility for the farm.'

He smiled sardonically at her, as though he knew just how hard she had found it to mutter the words.

'That's what neighbours are for. Your father would have done the same thing for me had our positions been reversed.' He pulled off his jacket, dropping it carelessly on to the table, and then checking and picking it up again. 'One special licence,' he told her withdrawing a piece of paper from an inner pocket. 'Special dispensation from the Bishop of Hawick. I went to see him today.'

'So we'll be married. . .'

'The day after tomorrow,' Blake told her. 'In Hexham, everything's arranged, the vicar. . .'

'A Church wedding?' Sapphire's head came up, her forehead creased in a frown. Somehow she had expected the ceremony to be conducted in the more mundane surroundings of a registry office.

'It seemed less public,' Blake told her carelessly. 'Have you told your boyfriend yet?'

Sapphire shook her head. 'No, but he's coming up for his car, I'll tell him then, it isn't the sort of news I could break over the 'phone.'

'He's going to get quite a shock.'

Why should she think she heard satisfaction beneath the cool words? 'It's only for a few months, once I've explained the situation to him. . .'

'He'll wait for you?' Blake supplied sardonically, 'Get your coat on and I'll take you back to Flaws, I've got to be up early in the morning. We've got to get the sheep down off the high pastures, the weather's about to change.'

They didn't speak again until Blake stopped his car outside the back door to Flaws Farm. For a moment as she unfastened her seat belt Sapphire panicked. What if he should try to kiss her again?

But apart from opening her door for her Blake didn't attempt to touch her. He walked with her across the cobbled yard, both of them stopping by the door.

'I won't see you tomorrow,' he told her, 'but I'll be round the morning after. Our appointment with the Vicar is for eleven o'clock, so I'll pick you up at ten.' Giving her a brief nod he turned away and walked back to the car. He had reversed out of the yard before Sapphire had managed to pull herself together sufficiently to open the back door.

What was the matter with her, she chided herself as she prepared for bed. Surely she hadn't wanted him to kiss her? Of course she hadn't. So why this curiously flat feeling; this niggly ache in her body that was all too dangerously familiar? Stop it, she cautioned herself as she slid into the cold bed. Stop thinking about him.

It was easier said than done, especially with twenty-four empty hours stretching ahead of her with nothing to fill them other than doubts about the wisdom of marrying Blake for a second time, no matter how altruistic the reasons.

She helped Mary with her chores, and spent the afternoon outdoors, but although she kept her hands busy she couldn't occupy her mind. Her father noticed her tension when she went to sit with him.

'Worrying about tomorrow?' he asked sympathetically, closing the book he had been reading.

'Blake is a fine man Sapphire,' he told her gently, 'I've always thought so. In fact in many ways I blame myself for the break-up of your marriage.'

When she started to protest he lifted his hand. 'I wanted you to marry Blake, even though he thought you were too young. He wanted to wait, but. . .'

'But you dangled the bait of this farm,' Sapphire interrupted briefly, 'and he couldn't resist it.' She bit her lip as she realised how cold and unloverlike her voice sounded. Deliberately trying to soften it, she added, 'But that's all over now, we're making a completely fresh start. We're both older and wiser.'

She couldn't bear to look at her father. His fragility still had the power to shock her, but even so her mind refused to accept that soon he would be gone from her.

Downstairs she found Mary busily baking. 'Blake just rang to confirm that he'll pick you up at ten tomorrow,' she said cheerfully. 'Having a day out?'

Her curiosity was only natural and Sapphire forced a smile. 'Yes . . . In fact you might as well know Mary, that Blake and I are going to give our marriage another try.' She couldn't look at the other woman. 'I suppose it took something like my father's . . . illness to show us both how we really felt.' That at least was true, even if Mary was hardly likely to interpret her words correctly. The other woman's face softened.

'Yes I know what you mean,' she agreed. 'So you'll be moving to Sefton House.'

'Yes.' Sapphire swallowed nervously. So far she hadn't let herself think about the intimacy of living in such close proximity to Blake. No matter how non-sexual their relationship was going to be; the thought made her stomach tense and knot in anxious apprehension. What was she frightened of for goodness sake? Not Blake. She already knew that he felt absolutely no desire for her, but last night he had talked about taking her home with him and making her truly his wife. Sapphire shivered. Those had been words; nothing more; words designed to keep her tense and apprehensive; and in her place. No, she had nothing to fear from Blake. Or from herself? Of course not. She had suffered the agony of loving him once, it was hardly likely to happen again.

CHAPTER FIVE

SHE and Blake were husband and wife again; Sapphire could hardly believe it. She glanced down at the gold band encircling her finger. It was the same ring that Blake had given her once before. She had been stunned when she saw it. Somehow she had never imagined Blake keeping it, never mind giving it back to her.

'It saved the bother of buying a new one,' he told her sardonically correctly following her chain of thought. He glanced at his watch flicking back his cuff in a manner that was achingly familiar. It shocked her that her mind should have stored and retained so many minute details about him. 'We'd better get back. I take it you don't want to go out and celebrate our reunion?'

'Can you think of any reason why I should?' Her voice was as cool as his, her eyes locking with the gold blaze that glittered over her too pale face. 'I've married you for one reason and one reason only Blake—my father's peace of mind, and just as soon as . . .' she gulped back the stinging tears that suddenly formed, '. . . just as soon as that reason no longer exists our marriage will be over.'

The silence that filled the car on the way back to the valley was not a comfortable one. Sapphire sat back in her seat, her head on the headrest, her face turned dismissively towards the window, and yet despite her determination to ignore Blake, she was acutely aware of him. Every time she closed her

eyes she saw his face; pictured the lean strength of
his hands on the steering wheel. For a moment,
unnervingly she even pictured those hands against
her skin, touching; stroking... Stop it, she
warned herself. Dear God what was happening to
her? Blake no longer possessed the power to affect
her in that way. She was completely over him and
the childish infatuation she had once had for him.

'We'll drive to Flaws Farm and pick up your
things first.' His cool voice broke into her
thoughts. 'I've got the vet coming out this
afternoon to look at the mare, so we won't linger.'

'The fact that we're married doesn't mean we
have to do everything together,' Sapphire pointed
out tartly, not liking the way he was taking
control. 'I can easily drive myself over to Flaws. In
fact,' she turned in her seat to look determinedly
at Blake, 'in view of my father's illness and the fact
that no-one knows that we've been divorced, I
think it would be quite acceptable for me to
remain at Flaws...'

'Maybe it would,' Blake agreed sardonically, 'if
your daughterly devotion wasn't a bit late in
coming, and I was prepared to agree. Oh no,
Sapphire,' he told her softly, 'I want you where I
can keep an eye on you. You're not running out
on me twice. Besides,' he added, 'if you don't come
back to Sefton House with me, your father's going
to get suspicious.'

His last words were undeniably true. Biting
down hard on her lip to prevent her vexation from
showing Sapphire turned back to stare out of her
window, relieved when she saw the familiar turn-
off for Flaws Valley. This tension between herself
and Blake wasn't something she remembered from

the past. Of course, she had always been aware of him; but surely never like this, with a nerve-rasping intensity that made her muscles ache from the strain she was imposing on them.

'You're back early.' Mary greeted them without any surprise, but of course as far as she was concerned she and Blake had merely had a morning out together. 'Are you staying for lunch?' Her question was addressed to Blake, but his arm tethered Sapphire to his side when she would have slipped out of the room. 'We haven't got time, I've got the vet coming this afternoon.' He released Sapphire to smile down at her, his eyes so warm and golden that his glance was like basking in the heat of the sun. 'I'll go up and see your father while you pack.'

He was gone before Sapphire could speak, leaving her to face Mary's raised eyebrows and expectant expression. Sapphire couldn't face her. 'I . . . I'm going back with Blake,' she said hesitantly, 'I . . . we. . . .'

'Your father will be pleased,' Mary assured her coming to her rescue. 'Look,' she added, 'why don't I make some coffee and then come upstairs and give you a hand with your packing. Not that you brought a lot with you.'

Sensing the speculation behind her words Sapphire said shakily. 'N . . . I had no idea then that Blake. . .'

'Still loved you?'

The words surprised her into a tense stillness, but mercifully Mary was too busily engaged in making the coffee to notice her startled response. It had been on the tip of her tongue to blurt out that Blake had never loved her, but fortunately she had caught the words back just in time.

It was over an hour before they were finally able to leave. Her father had been so pleased by their news. Sighing Sapphire tried to settle herself in the car, telling herself that her sacrifice must surely have been made worthwhile by her father's pleasure.

'I'm going to have to leave you to find your own way about,' Blake told her tensely when he stopped the car in his own farmyard. 'I want to have a word with the shepherd before the vet arrives. You'll have to make yourself up a bed I'm afraid—unless of course you prefer to share mine.' The last words were accompanied by a cynical smile.

'Hardly,' Sapphire told him crisply, 'I'm no masochist, Blake; nor am I a naive seventeen-year-old any longer.'

'No,' he agreed bitterly, and for a moment Sapphire wondered at the deeply intense timbre of his voice and the drawn expression tensing his face, before dismissing her impressions as false ones and berating herself for allowing her imagination to work overtime. Blake had no reason to feel bitter—unlike her.

As she let herself into the kitchen she was struck by the fact that despite, or perhaps because of its gleaming appearance the room seemed oddly sterile; not like a home at all. The mellow wooden cabinets which should have imparted a warm glow, looked too much like a glossy, cold advertisement; there were no warm, baking smells to tantalise or tempt. Blake's aunt had made her own bread, she remembered with unexpected nostalgia, and she remembered this kitchen best filled with its warmly fragrant scent. Of course if the smell of freshly baked bread was all it took to bring the place alive, she was more than capable of supplying that herself. Her culinary efforts so much despised by Blake's aunt had improved rapidly in the security of her own small home. Alan often asked her to cook for important clients and among their circle of friends she had quite a reputation as a first-rate hostess. Alan approved of her domestic talents; Alan! Her body tensed. What was he going to say when he heard about all this? She could well lose him. Why was she not more concerned at the prospect; after all she had been planning to marry him? Pushing aside the thought she opened the kitchen door and stepped into the square parquet-floored hall.

On the plate rack encircling the hall were the plates she remembered from the early days of her marriage, the smooth cream walls otherwise clean and bare. The parquet floor glistened in the bright March sunshine, but the table was empty of its customary bowl of flowers and she found she missed their bright splash of colour. Whatever her other faults Blake's aunt had been a first rate housewife, and she had obviously learned something from her Sapphire thought wryly, noticing the thin film of dust beginning to form on the hall table. The rich reds and blues of the traditional stair carpet carried her eye upwards. The house had six bedrooms and two bathrooms; a more than adequate supply for two people. Did Blake still occupy the master bedroom? It had been re-decorated especially for them before their marriage she remembered, in soft peaches and blues that Blake had told her he had chosen with her eyes in mind. Her mouth curled into a sardonic smile. And to think she had been fool enough to believe him. The door handle turned easily under her fingers, but she stood still once it was opened. Everything was just as she remembered it; everything was clean and neat, but the room gave the impression of being unused.

'Re-living old memories?' Blake's voice was harshly discordant making her whirl round in shock.

She said the first thing that came into her mind. 'It doesn't look used.'

'It isn't.' His voice was still harsh, his eyes fiercely golden as they all but pinned her where she stood. 'Let's face it,' he added cynically, 'the memories it holds aren't precisely those I want to take to bed with me every night. I sleep in my old room, but you can have this one if you wish.'

His old room. Unwillingly her eyes were drawn along the corridor to the room she knew he meant. She had only been in it once. She had come with a message from her father and finding the kitchen empty and hearing Blake's voice had hurried upstairs. He had emerged from his room just as she reached it, a towel wrapped round lean hips, his body still damp from his shower. She hadn't been able to take her eyes off him, she remembered sardonically; and neither had she been able to speak. Blake had drawn her inside the room closing the door. 'What is it little girl,' he had asked tauntingly, 'haven't you ever seen a man before?' She had turned to flee but he had caught her, kissing her with what she had interpreted as fierce passion but which in reality could only have been play-acting. . .

'Sapphire, are you all right?' His voice dragged her back to the present.

'Fine,' she told him in a clipped voice. 'I might as well use this room. The woman who comes up from the village, when. . .'

'Three days a week, if you feel you need her more then arrange it. Don't worry,' he added sardonically, watching her, 'I don't expect you to soil your ladylike hands with housework, or cooking.' If anything his mouth curled even more cynically. 'I have too much respect for my stomach for that. I came up to tell you that I've brought your cases in. Once the vet's been, I've got to go out and check one of the fences, some of the sheep were found on the road. . .'

He disappeared, leaving Sapphire standing by the open door, her face still scarlet from his insults about her cooking. So he thought she was still the same useless, timid child he had first married, did he? Well she would show him.

Returning upstairs, Sapphire quickly changed into her jeans and an old tee-shirt. A thorough inspection of the kitchen cupboards revealed the fact that they were surprisingly well stocked and within an hour of Blake's exit she had a large bowl of dough rising in the warmth of the upstairs airing cupboard—a trick she had learned in her London flat which lacked the large warming compartment of the old-fashioned stove at home.

She heard the vet arrive while she was making the pastry for Beef Wellington, but continued with her self-imposed task. Blake would soon discover that she was not the timid child she had once been, and she wouldn't have been human, she told herself, if she didn't take pleasure from imagining his surprise at the discovery.

She had half-expected Blake to bring the vet in for a cup of tea after he had inspected that mare—it was a cold day, and she was sure the older man would have welcomed a warming drink, but instead when they emerged from the barn Blake walked with him to his Range Rover. The two men stood talking for a few minutes and then the vet climbed into his vehicle and Blake turned back towards the stable, disappearing inside.

Sapphire had just put her loaves in the oven when the 'phone rang. Wiping her floury hands on a towel she picked up the receiver, recognising Miranda's slightly shrill voice the moment she heard it.

'Is Blake there?' the other woman demanded imperiously. 'I want to speak to him—urgently.'

'He's in the barn at the moment,' Sapphire responded coolly, suppressing the urge to slam the receiver down. 'If you'd like to hold on for a moment I'll go and get him.'

The interior of the barn, so dark after the bright sunlit afternoon was temporarily blinding. Sapphire was peripherally aware of the familiar barn sounds; the mare shuffling restlessly in her stall, the scent of hay, the rustling sound it made. As her eyes grew accustomed to the gloom she stepped forward calling Blake's name.

'Up here,' he called back, making her start tensely and peer upwards into the dimness of the upper hayloft.

'There's a 'phone call for you,' Sapphire told him curtly, not wanting to think she had come looking for him on her own account. 'Miranda.'

'I'll have to ring her back.' Blake was frowning as he turned back into the interior of the loft, and although she knew she was being foolish Sapphire couldn't quite control the sudden leap of her senses as she caught a glimpse of the tawny skin of his chest where his shirt had come unfastened. Enough, she berated herself, as she walked blindly towards the door. 'You don't even like the man—you loathe him, so how can you possibly . . . feel desire for him?' Somehow the words insinuated themselves into her mind and wouldn't go away, making her face up to the truth. Blake still had the power to disturb her; still held a sexual appeal for her, which although it had nothing to do with love, or indeed any genuine worthwhile emotion, did, nonetheless, hold a dangerously potent allure.

Deep in thought Sapphire recoiled with pain as she cannoned into one of the posts supporting the upper floor, the intensity of the unexpected pain almost robbing her of breath as she stumbled backwards.

She was aware of sounds behind her, of Blake's peremptory command and then the firm strength of his arm supporting her against his body as she slowly crumpled.

'Sapphire, are you all right?'

His voice was a roughly urgent mutter somewhere above her left ear; the heat of his body against her back drowning out her earlier pain and replacing it with a dangerous languor that reinforced every one of her earlier thoughts.

'Sapphire?'

This time the urgency in Blake's voice compelled her to make some response. 'I'm fine,' she told him shakily, 'it was just the shock... It took my breath away.'

'I know the feeling.' She could feel the reverberations of his words rumbling in his chest, but the dry tone in which they were uttered made her lift her head and turn round the better to study his face.

'Can't you feel what having you in my arms does to me?' he murmured rawly. 'I'd almost forgotten it was possible to feel like this.'

Sapphire didn't need to ask 'to feel like what?' Her own treacherous body was already reacting shamelessly to Blake's proximity. You fool, she protested inwardly, he doesn't care any more about you than he did before; it's just another act, another scene of the charade he insists we play. He doesn't want you.

But Blake's body was telling her otherwise. More experienced now than she had been at seventeen, she could clearly read the tell-tale signs; in the dim light of the barn his eyes glittered dark gold, searching her face as he cupped her jaw with one hand and turned her round to face him. There was a tension in his body that was betrayed by the fine tremor of his muscles and the harsh control he exercised over his breathing.

The knowledge that she had aroused him was infinitely exciting; dangerously intoxicating, so much so that she was drunk on it. There could be no other explanation for the suicidal desire she suddenly experienced to trace the deep vee of Blake's open shirt with the tip of one finger, nor for giving into it.

Apart from one deep inhaled breath Blake kept absolutely still. His skin felt warm and surprisingly vulnerable, the difference in texture between his skin and the crispness of his dark chest hair deeply erotic. She had never touched him like this in the past; had never dared to initiate any intimacy between them. A pulse thudded at the base of his throat, his fingers tensing into her waist as he looked down at her.

'Sapphire!'

Her name seemed to well up from the very depths of his soul, spilling into the silence of the barn as a tormented groan. Her shocked senses barely had time to register it before the hard fingers cupping her jaw were tilting her face up and his mouth was consuming hers, burning it with a kiss of such fierce intensity that her senses took fire from it, liquid heat running moltenly through her veins, making her melt into him with a feverish need to meld with him and become part of him.

When his tongue stroked her lips, coaxing them apart Sapphire surrendered willingly, an ache that was partly desire and partly pain flowering to life inside her. Never once had he kissed her like this before; like a man who had hungered desperately for the feel of her mouth beneath his; who burned with a totally male desire to conquer and possess.

His free hand stroked down her body, finding the soft curve of her breast his thumb finding the newly burgeoning peak and caressing it with a feverish intensity that was echoed in the taut tension of his body.

Everything in her that was feminine yielded beneath the force of such a rawly masculine need and as though his body sensed the responsiveness of hers, Blake slid his hand beneath her tee-shirt, searching for and finding the aroused swell of her breast.

Which of them made the small murmur of satisfaction Sapphire didn't know, all she did know was that by the time Blake's mouth left hers, to investigate the creamy curve of her throat, she was totally acquiescent; mutely encouraging the exploration of warm male lips and slightly calloused male hands.

'Sapphire if you don't stop me now, I'm going to end up making love to you where we stand.'

Blake groaned the words into her skin, using his superior strength to urge her against the hard arousal of his body, muttering thick words of pleasure as his hands slid down to her hips, moulding her against him, but his words had penetrated through the dizzying heat of desire welling up inside her and Sapphire pulled away. He released her almost immediately, the desire she had seen so recently in his face draining away to be replaced by sardonic comprehension.

'You forgot who I was, is that it?' he taunted, watching the emotions chase one another across her mobile face. 'You forgot that I wasn't your precious boyfriend, is that what you're going to tell me? Well I'll save you the trouble,' he told her. 'That was *me* you responded to Sapphire, *me* who set you on fire; *me* who you wanted to make love to.'

'Oh yes you did,' he insisted when she tried to speak. 'You wanted me Sapphire, whether you're honest to admit it or not.'

'Whatever there once was between us is gone,' Sapphire protested, bitterly ·aware that he was right; she *had* wanted him and with an intensity that, now that she had herself under control again, shocked her.

'But you can't deny that you responded to me,' Blake pressed softly, watching her, making her feel trapped and tormented.

'I can't deny that I responded to your *masculinity*,' Sapphire agreed in a face-saving bid... 'I'm a woman now Blake, with all the desires and needs that that implies.' Heavens was this really her saying this? Inwardly she was trembling, praying that he wouldn't see through her pitiful attempt to deny the effect he had on her.

'Meaning that you would have responded to any man in the same way?' Blake asked her sardonically. 'I don't think so, Sapphire. In fact, judging by your response to me, there must be something lacking in your boyfriend's lovemaking. You responded to me as though you were starving for...'

'Stop it,' Sapphire interrupted his cruel speech. 'I won't listen to this, Blake.' She hurried to the barn door, wanting only to escape from him and the turbulence of her own emotions, completely forgetting the original purpose of her journey to the barn, until she got back to the kitchen and found the receiver still on the table. There was no-one at the other end and so she replaced it, busying herself in the kitchen, trying to find some balm to her disordered senses in the warm scent of baking bread that filled the room, but instead only able to remember the rough sensuality of Blake's mouth on hers; the urgent caress of his hands on her body; the unashamed arousal of his as he kissed and caressed her, but no, she mustn't think of these things. She must concentrate instead of remembering why she was here; how Blake had trapped her.

She was busily clearing away the remnants of pastry from the table when Blake walked in, checking on the threshold, frowning slightly as the warmly rich scent of her baking filled his nostrils. She ought to have been pleased by the startled expression on his face, but instead all she could think of was the way his mouth had felt against her own, and it took an almost physical effort to draw her gaze away from the slightly moist fullness of his lower lip.

'Bread?' he quizzed her, obviously surprised.

'Alan liked me to bake it for him,' Sapphire responded, knowing that she was deliberately invoking Alan's name as though it were a charm which had the ability to destroy Blake's powerful pull on her senses. Blake's face hardened immediately, as he strode across the kitchen and picked up the 'phone. Watching him punch in a series of numbers, so quickly that he must know them by heart, Sapphire was pierced by a feeling of desolation so acute that it terrified her. She mustn't become emotionally involved with Blake again. She had travelled that road once and knew all too well where it led; she wasn't going to travel it again.

Her desolation turned to sick pain as she heard him say Miranda's name. The other woman must have said something because Blake laughed, a deeply sensual sound that stirred up the tiny hairs on the back of Sapphire's nape, making her spine tingle.

'No, she must have forgotten to give me the

message,' Sapphire heard him say, his eyes hard, his gaze unwavering splintering her with pain as she turned to face him. 'Umm . . . well how about dinner tonight? Yes I'll pick you up.'

Sapphire turned away, Blake was taking Miranda out to dinner? She glanced at the 'fridge where the pastry and fillet steak she had prepared for their evening meal lay, and her mouth compressed in a bitter line. Hadn't she already learned her lesson?

By the time Blake had replaced the receiver she had decided what she would do. Let Blake take his . . . mistress out to dinner if he wished, but she wasn't going to sit at home, moping, waiting for him. She would go over to Flaws and spend the evening with Mary and her father.

It wasn't until she heard the door close behind Blake that she realised that she had been holding her breath. Her lungs ached with the strain she was imposing on them, her body so tense that her muscles were almost locked.

Why on earth had she allowed Blake to kiss and touch her as he had? And why had she responsed to him so . . . so ardently. She didn't love him any longer; but she still desired him; part of her still felt the old attraction; *that* must be the explanation. Like an amputee suffering pain from a limb that no longer existed she was still experiencing the pangs of her youthful love for Blake even though that love had long ago died.

Sapphire was in her room when Blake went out; she had gone there, deliberately avoiding him, and only emerged once she had heard his car engine die away.

Despite the fact that the heating was on the house felt slightly chilly—a sure sign that the threat of bad weather hadn't gone. In the living room a basket of logs stood on the hearth of the open fire, and Sapphire glanced longingly at them, acknowledging that it was pointless lighting a fire just for herself, especially when she didn't intend staying in. Why, when she knew where Blake had gone; when she knew how he had manipulated her, did her imagination insist on filling her mind with pictures of Blake as she had always wanted him to be rather than as he was; of herself at his side; their children upstairs asleep while they sat side by side by the warm glow of the fire; happy and content. Suppressing a sigh Sapphire walked into the kitchen, still redolent with the fragrance of her newly baked bread. On the table one of her loaves stood on the breadboard surrounded by crumbs. Blake had obviously cut himself a slice, and probably given himself indigestion she thought wryly, touching the still warm loaf.

Knowing that if she remained alone any longer in the house she would only brood, Sapphire picked up her jacket and headed for the Land Rover. Spending the evening with her father would stop her thinking about the past; about useless might-have-beens, she decided firmly, as she swung herself up into the utilitarian vehicle. She was just about to start the motor when a sound from the barn stopped her. Tensing she listened, wondering if she was imagining things, and then she heard it again; the shrill, unmistakable whinny of a horse in pain.

Blake's mare! But he had told her that the vet had said she probably wouldn't start to foal for at least twenty-four hours. Frowning Sapphire glanced towards the barn door, her conscience prodding her to get out of the Land Rover and go and investigate. She wasn't a stranger to animal birth; and as she hurried into the barn, snapping on the light, her experienced eye quickly took in the mare's distressed state and knew that the vet had been wrong. By the looks of her the mare was already in labour.

Despite her long years in London old habits re-asserted themselves. Soothing the mare as best she could, Sapphire left her to race back to the house. To her relief the vet's wife answered the 'phone almost immediately. Quickly Sapphire explained the position.

'The vet isn't here,' she told Sapphire, 'but I know where he is. I'll 'phone him and let him know the position. I know he'll be with you just as soon as he can. Are you able to get in touch with Blake?' she asked worriedly, 'I know how much he thinks of that mare. . .'

It wasn't hard for Sapphire to find Miranda's telephone number, but she hesitated before dialling it. As she had half-expected, there was no answer. She ought to have felt a savage satisfaction that Blake was being repaid for his duplicity, but all she could feel was a growing concern for the mare, and concern at her own ability to handle the situation. The shepherd who might have been able to help was out on the hills with his flock; her father was far too ill to help and Mary. . . Mary was a trained nurse, Sapphire remembered excitedly, picking up the phone again and punching in the numbers quickly.

Mary listened while she explained the situation.

'I'll be right over,' she assured Sapphire. 'The vet may not be long, but it's better to be safe than sorry. This won't be the first birth I've attended bya long chalk.'

While she was waiting, more to keep herself busy than anything else Sapphire boiled water and scalded the buckets, finding carbolic soap, and a pack of clean, unused rope. If for some reason the foal was turned the wrong way they might need the rope. Hurriedly she tried to think of anything else they might need, rushing out into the yard when she heard the sound of a vehicle. To her disappointment it was Mary and not the vet who alighted from the Range Rover.

'You've done well,' she approved as she followed Sapphire into the barn. 'But where's Blake?'

'He had to go out,' Sapphire avoided her eyes. 'I haven't been able to reach him.'

Fortunately Mary was too busy examining the mare to hear the slight hesitation in her voice.

'The foal's turned into the breech position,' Mary explained, fulfilling Sapphire's own fears. 'I'll try and turn it, can you hold the mare's head, try and soothe her?'

Her father had once told Sapphire that she had a way with animals, and Sapphire prayed that he might be right as she softly coaxed the nervous mare, talking to her in soothing whispers.

'This isn't her first foal,' Mary commented, 'but she's very nervous.'

'Missing Blake, I expect,' Sapphire murmured absently. 'Are you going to be able to turn it?'

'I think so.' Mary's face was strained with the effort of concentrating on her task, and Sapphire felt herself willing her to succeed.

'There . . . I think that's done it. Good girl,' she soothed the mare, adding to Sapphire, 'I think we can let nature take its course now, although I hope the birth won't be too protracted, she's already suffered a lot of pain.'

As the birth pangs rippled through the mare's swollen belly Sapphire found herself tensing in sympathy with her, and yet the mare did seem more relaxed as though she knew that they were there to help her.

'Quick, Sapphire, look.' Mary's voice was exultant as she pointed to the foal's head as it emerged from its mother's body. Deftly she moved to assist the mare, Sapphire immediately moving to help, remembering how she had assisted her father in the past.

The foal was a tiny bundle of stick-like limbs on the straw at its mother's feet when they heard the sound of a vehicle outside.

A door slammed and the vet came hurrying in bringing a gust of cold air with him, his anxious frown relaxing into a smile as he saw the foal. 'Well, well what have we here?' he asked gently, quickly examining the mare, nodding with approval as he inspected the foal.

'I'm sorry I couldn't get here before—an emergency at Low Head farm, but you seem to have managed well enough without me.' His smile was for Sapphire, but she shook her head, directing his attention to Mary. 'Without Mary's help I couldn't have done it.'

'The foal had turned,' Mary explained, 'but fortunately he was small enough for me to turn back.'

'Umm, quick thinking on your part to send for

Mary,' the vet praised Sapphire, 'but where's Blake?'

'He had to go out.' Sapphire repeated the explanation she had given Mary.

'Lucky for him and the mare that you were here.' His eyes were curious as he inspected her, and Sapphire wondered if he knew that she was Blake's wife, and that they were back together again.

It was another two hours before Sapphire could crawl into bed. She had made supper for Mary and the vet, who had pronounced both mother and foal to be in perfect health, and by the time they had gone she had been almost too tired to sink into the hot bath she had run for herself. As she pulled the quilt up round her ears she glanced at her watch. One o'clock, and Blake still wasn't back. A bitter pain invaded her body. Was he at this very moment making love to Miranda, kissing her with the barely restrained passion he had shown her earlier in the day? They had not been lovers he had said to her, and for a moment she had believed him, but surely his actions tonight proved that he had lied?

She closed her eyes, willing herself to sleep. She *wasn't* going to lie here awake, wondering where he was, waiting for him to return as she had done so often in the past.

CHAPTER SIX

A SURPRISE awaited Sapphire when she opened her eyes the following morning. It was the clarity of the light in her bedroom that first alerted her, and padding across the room on bare feet she flung back the curtains, bemused to see the white blanket of snow that must have fallen during the night. Everything was so quiet; the air so crystal clear it was almost like wine. She frowned; where was Blake? Had he even returned? She padded back to bed, picking up her watch and nearly dropping it as she realised how long she had overslept. It was gone ten o'clock!

Showering quickly she ran downstairs and opened the kitchen door. The room was empty but there was evidence that Blake had had some breakfast. The aroma of coffee hung tantalisingly in the air making her aware of her thirst. Deftly she moved about the kitchen going to stand by the window as she waited for the coffee to filter into the jug. The snow lay surprisingly deep in the yard, criss-crossed with footmarks plus those of a dog. Of course, the sheep! Sapphire gnawed at her bottom lip. Attractive as though the snow was to look at it could spell disaster for any unwary farmer. She remembered her father's shepherd telling her that he had expected this weather. Had Blake got the ewes down to the lower pastures? If not there was every danger that the new lambs would be lost beneath the huge drifts Sapphire knew could form on the bleak mountain tops. Without consciously making any decision she found herself searching in the porch for a pair of suitable Wellingtons, mentally ticking off all that she would need if she was to be any help to the men. She could follow their tracks through the snow without any difficulty. Perhaps if she took them hot coffee and tea . . .

Fifteen minutes later Sapphire tramped through the farmyard, following the clearly defined footprints upwards. The snow had frozen to a crisp crust, her laboured breath made white plumes in the sharp morning air. At another time she would have found the atmosphere invigorating, but right now she was too concerned about the sheep to really enjoy the delights of the morning.

The baaing of the sheep and the sharp yelps of the dogs reached her first, carrying easily on the clear air, and she expelled her breath on a faint sigh of relief. Obviously some of the sheep at least had been brought down to the lower meadows. As she followed the footprints along a dry-stone wall Sapphire caught her first glimpse of her quarry, a rough shelter had been constructed in one of the fields, and men were busy unbaling hay from a tractor. The field sloped away slightly offering some protection from the wind and drifts, and as she got nearer Sapphire recognised her father's shepherd, busily at work. The other men she also vaguely recognised as general farmhands attached to Blake's farm whom he had no doubt taken from their other tasks to help with the all-important job of saving the sheep.

Tam recognised her face, a weary grin splitting his weathered face as he hailed her.

'I've brought you something hot to drink,' Sapphire called out as soon as she was close enough, adding anxiously, 'How's it going? The ewes. . .'

'Brought most of them down yesterday,' Tam informed her. 'Blake's gone looking for the rest of the flock. Shouldn't have too much of a problem with my Laddie to help him. Fine sheepdog.'

'Anything I can do to help?' Sapphire asked, handing out the thermos flasks and cups.

'No. I reckon everything's under control. Luckily Blake was running your dad's flock with his own, so we shouldn't have too many casualties. If this weather had come another two weeks on we could have been in trouble—the first ewes are due to start lambing then.'

'You don't think it will last then?' Sapphire asked, studying the snow-covered landscape.

Tam shook his head. 'Not more than three or four days, and we were prepared for it.' He nodded in the direction of the new shelter and the bales of hay. 'Blake knows what he's doing all right.' There was approval in his voice and Sapphire turned away, not wanting the shepherd to see her own bitter resentment. What time had Blake come home last night? He could have had precious little sleep she thought revengefully. Had he arrived before the snow came or had the fact that she had not heard him been due to the fact that it had muffled his return?

What did it matter? It was no business of hers how he spent his time, or whose bed he shared.

She waited until the men had finished their drinks before gathering up the empty flasks.

'I'll keep this one for Blake,' Tam offered taking

a half-full one from her and screwing on the top. 'He'll be fair frozen by the time he gets back.'

'Is he up there alone?' Sapphire frowned when the shepherd nodded. 'Is that wise?'

'Blake knows what he's doing.'

Tam had been right, Sapphire reflected several hours later when a noise in the yard alerted her to Blake's return. Snow clung to his thick protective jacket and the cuffs of his boots, his skin burned by the icy cold wind. She hadn't known whether to prepare a meal or not—there was still the Beef Wellington to cook from last night, and she had spent what was left of the morning making a nourishing hot soup, thinking that if Blake didn't return she could take it out to the men in flasks.

She had also been in to inspect the new foal, now standing proudly on all four spindly legs while his mother looked on in benign approval.

As Blake crossed the yard the 'phone rang. It was her father calling to enquire about the sheep. 'Everything's under control, Dad,' she assured him. 'Blake had already got the ewes down to the lower pastures and he's been up to the top to bring the rest down.'

'Yes, Mary told me I didn't need to worry, but old habits die hard.'

The kitchen door opened as she replied, and she could hear the sound of Blake tugging off his boots. 'Blake's back now,' she told her father, 'would you like to speak to him?'

'No, I know myself what it's like. He'll be frozen to the marrow and tired out—the last thing he'll feel like is talking to me. I'll speak to him later when he's thawed out.'

'Who was that?'

She hadn't heard Blake cross the floor in his stockinged feet and whirled round apprehensively. Exhaustion tautened the bone structure of his face, dimming the gold of his eyes to tawny brown. White flecks of snow clung to his hair and jumper.

'My father. Is it snowing again?'

'Trying to. God I'm tired. Is there any hot water?'

'Plenty. Would you like something to eat?' She saw his eyebrows lift and mockery invade his eyes. 'Quite the devoted wife today aren't we? What brought about this metamorphosis?'

'Nothing . . . there hasn't been one.' Sapphire retorted flatly cursing herself for her momentary weakness. 'I just thought. . .'

'Yes, I'm sorry.' Strong dark fingers raked through his already tousled hair. 'That was uncalled for—put it down to sheer male. . .' His glance studied her slim body in its covering of jeans and sweater and he grimaced faintly before adding bluntly, 'frustration. . . Deprivation of physical satisfaction does tend to make me behave like a churlish brute, and I haven't even thanked you for your midwifery last night. . .'

'Mary's the one you should thank,' Sapphire told him, turning away and busying herself filling the kettle. She wanted to scream at him that she didn't want to know the details about his relationship with Miranda or about his physical hunger for her. Was that why he had made love to *her* so intensely yesterday? In anticipation of holding Miranda in his arms? The thought made her feel physically sick, but what was even more shocking was the knowledge that she could feel so strongly and primitively about a man for whom she had already told herself she felt only the echoes of an old physical desire.

'Is something wrong?'

She could feel him approaching and tensed. 'No, nothing.' She couldn't bear him to come anywhere near her right now, not when her far too active mind was picturing him with Miranda, kissing and caressing her. The handle of the mug she had been holding in her hand snapped under the intensity of her grip, the mug falling to the floor where it shattered into fragments.

'No . . . don't. Leave it.' Her voice was sharper than she had intended, almost shrill in its intensity and she prayed that Blake wouldn't recognise the near hysteria edging up under it. 'You haven't got anything on your feet,' she added weakly. 'You go and have your bath and I'll clean it up. Are you hungry now, or can you wait an hour or so?'

'I can wait.' He too sounded clipped and terse, but Sapphire couldn't look at him to read the reason in his expression. Instead she waited until she heard the door close behind him and then carefully skirting the broken china went to get a brush and pan to clear up the mess.

She was putting the Beef Wellington into the oven when she heard Blake call out something from upstairs. Reacting without thinking Sapphire hurried up them, coming to an abrupt halt outside his bedroom door, wondering whether to knock or simply walk in. The dilemma was solved for her as Blake pulled the door open. He had taken off his sweater and shirt, and his skin gleamed silky bronze beneath the electric light. Her breathing, which hadn't been in the slightest affected by her dash upstairs, now suddenly constricted, her heart thudding heavily its beats reverberating through her body.

'I've scraped my back against a wall. I think the skin's broken.' Blake turned his back to her as he spoke and Sapphire saw the patch of broken skin, slightly swollen and discoloured with dried blood.

Farm accidents no matter how minor always had to be properly attended to; that was one of the first rules Sapphire had ever learned and she knew better than to accuse Blake of being too fussy in wanting the graze attended to. Neither would he be able to deal with it himself, positioned as it was just below his shoulder blade.

'I'll go and get some antiseptic and cotton wool. Your tetanus shots are up to date I hope?'

'Do you?' Blake grimaced sardonically, flexing his shoulder as he moved away from her, as though the muscles pained him. 'Funny, I had the distinct impression you'd like nothing better than to see me suffer.'

'Don't.' Sapphire whispered the protest, her face paper white, remembering the stories Tam had told her as a child about farm workers who had died from the dreaded 'lockjaw'. Fortunately, with his back to her Blake couldn't see her betraying expression, nor question her as to why she should feel such concern for someone she purportedly hated.

Why did she? She was forced to ask herself the question as she hurried into the bathroom for antiseptic and cotton-wool. There was nothing personal in her concern, she assured herself, she would have reacted the same way no matter who was involved. But she would not have reacted so intensely to the sight of anyone else's half-naked body; she would not have wanted to stretch out and touch the bronze skin and hard muscles, excitement gripping her by the throat as she visualised that same body. . . No . . . she was over all that. She no longer loved Blake, but for some reason her senses were playing cruel tricks on her, tormenting her with mental images of herself in Blake's arms; of Blake making love to her with all the fierce passion she suspected lay beneath his sardonic exterior.

Fool, fool, she berated herself as she hurried back to the stark, functional bedroom Blake had chosen for his own occupation. As she walked in she noticed that the bed looked untidy and rumpled. When she had dealt with Blake's wound she would change the sheets and tidy up a bit. *Very wifely*, the inner cynical voice she had come to dread mocked her, *but it won't make him want you.* I don't want him to want me. The denial seemed to reverberate inside her skull, and then as though it knew how paper-frail it was that other voice taunted softly, *Liar*.

'Sapphire?' Blake's curt voice cut across her thoughts. 'Are you all right?' He was frowning, his eyes sharpening to vivid gold as they searched her face.

'I'm not going to faint at the sight of a drop of your precious blood if that's what you think,' Sapphire responded tartly, adding with a calm she was far from feeling. 'While you're having your bath I'll change the bed for you. You'd better sit down on it, otherwise I'll never be able to reach the graze.'

'If you just clean it up for now,' Blake suggested, 'that should do the trick.'

'It will need a dressing on it,' Sapphire protested.

'Which will get soaked through the moment I get in the bath.'

'Then I'll put it on when you've finished,' Sapphire told him tartly, complaining, 'Honestly Blake, I never thought you of all people would be so irresponsible.'

'Perhaps I'm just testing to see exactly how deep your hatred of me really is,' Blake taunted back.

Sapphire compressed her lips. 'I'm not a child any more, Blake,' she reminded him. 'No matter what my personal feelings for you are, I wouldn't want to see you take the risk of getting a bad infection through a neglected skin wound.'

'Which doesn't really answer my question does it?'

'Sit down,' Sapphire instructed, ignoring his probing comment. 'This will sting,' she warned him as he sat down on the edge of the bed with his back to her. His skin looked so warm and inviting that it took all the self-control she possessed not to reach out and caress it.

'And won't you just enjoy it,' Blake muttered under his breath, tensing slightly as Sapphire applied the antiseptic soaked pad to his skin, gently cleaning the graze, until the blood flowed cleanly from it.

She let it flow for a few seconds, and then quickly stemmed it with fresh antiseptic, hiding a faint smile as Blake winced.

'Give me a shout when you're ready,' she told him when she had finished, 'and I'll come up and put a dressing on it for you. It should start to heal by morning.'

'Yes, nurse,' Blake mocked, getting up off the bed and momentarily making her feel at a distinct disadvantage as he towered over her. 'Taking a risk aren't you?' he drawled, watching her. For a moment Sapphire thought he meant the temptation she had exposed herself to in being so close to him, and her face flamed until he added softly, 'Isn't it a well known fact that patients always fall for their nurses?'

'In that case I think I'm pretty safe,' Sapphire responded, struggling to appear calmly unconcerned. 'After all I already know how you feel about me, don't I?'

Blake walked out without responding, and when she heard the bathroom door close behind him Sapphire got up and went to the large, old-fashioned airing cupboard situated on the landing to get clean sheets for his bed.

She worked methodically, changing the sheets, tidying up automatically, filling the laundry basket with the items of discarded clothing she found scattered round the room. Blake was basically a tidy man and there was nothing really in the starkly furnished room apart from his clothes that had his stamp of possession on it. If anything the room was rather bleak, she thought, studying it, almost monk-like. Mocking herself for her thoughts Sapphire carried the laundry out on to the landing. Blake was no monk, as she had seen last night.

She had just finished preparing the table when Blake called. Guessing that he would probably be tired she had decided that they might as well eat in the kitchen. It was warm and cosy enough and the table was large enough to seat an entire family, never mind merely two adults.

This time she walked into Blake's room without thinking, coming to an abrupt halt as she realised that he was nude. Of the two of them she was the one to be embarrassed she recognised angrily, as Blake merely grinned mockingly at her, taking his time in reaching for the towel that lay discarded on the bed.

'Why the outraged expression?' he demanded calmly. 'I can't be the first naked man you've seen.'

He was the only one, but Sapphire wasn't going to tell him that. 'Hardly,' she lied, shrugging aside the frisson of awareness the sight of his naked body had given her.

'And we are married. . .'

'Maybe, but it isn't the sort of marriage that involves parading around naked in front of one another.'

'What a pity.' Genuine amusement glinted in Blake's eyes as he teased her, and Sapphire had to fight against responding, against remembering how much joy there had been in loving him before she discovered the bitter truth. Blake had always been able to make her laugh, and even now she could feel the corners of her mouth twitching in response to his droll expression. The towel was firmly in place around his hips now, but to her chagrin that didn't stop Sapphire from visualising the taut shape of masculine buttocks and long hard thighs.

'Something smells good.' Blake's voice jerked her out of her reverie, and Sapphire bent her head to hide her guilty flush of colour. What on earth would he think if he knew what had been in her mind?

Fortunately he didn't, she assured herself as she gestured to the bed and suggested that he sit on it. This time she didn't allow herself to dwell on the supple texture of his skin or the masculine formation of muscle and bone that lay beneath it, finishing her self-imposed task with a haste she was surprised Blake didn't pick up on.

When the dressing was in place, she stepped away from him, tensing nervously as his fingers curled round her arm, preventing her from moving.

'Blake, let me go.' Her voice sounded sharp and nervous even to her own ears, and her anxiety increased when Blake refused to accede to her demand.

'I haven't rewarded you yet,' he told her softly, the hard grip of his fingers pulling her inexorably closer to him. 'All ministering angels deserve a reward, don't you agree?'

Whatever she might have said was lost as she felt the warm heat of Blake's body. She put out a hand to push him away, but the sensation of warm, sensuously silken male skin beneath her fingertips was so intoxicating that her resistance melted.

Dimly she was aware of Blake pulling her down on to his lap, and of the single bed creaking protestingly under their double weight.

She struggled to pull away out of his constraining arms, but Blake simply toppled her over on to the bed, imprisoning her against it with the superior weight of his body. His thighs pinned her lower body to the mattress, his chest hard against the softness of her breasts.

Sapphire felt vulnerable and helpless and yet the

sensations coursing through her veins and along her nerve endings whispered sensuously of pleasurable excitement rather than fear. Even so, she felt moved to protest shakily, 'Blake, let me get up, the dinner. . .'

Soft laughter brushed against her skin. 'Right now I'm hungry for more than just food.'

'Then perhaps you ought to give Miranda a ring,' Sapphire suggested tartly, struggling to push him away. She was glad she had said that, until that moment she had been dangerously close to giving way to the insiduous pull of her too vulnerable senses.

'Why should I need another man's wife, when I've got one of my own?' Blake countered outrageously, following her squirming movements and refusing to let her escape. His towel, Sapphire realised, had become dislodged, and weakening darts of pleasure relaxed her muscles into a sensuous lethargy as she felt her body reacting to the male provocation of Blake's body.

'Kiss me, Sapphire.'

She looked at him with desire-hazed eyes, barely comprehending the softly whispered command as she fought to subdue the treacherous impulses of her body.

'No.' She mumbled the denial huskily, knowing that it was far more than a kiss that Blake wanted from her. She wouldn't, she couldn't play substitute for Miranda.

'Yes.' The silky affirmation was whispered against her lips, the warmth of Blake's breath stirring to life a thousand tiny drumming pulses. Against her will Sapphire felt her mouth soften, her breathing suddenly ragged as Blake touched its soft contours with the tip of his tongue, expertly teasing light kisses into the corners, tormentingly stroking her sensitised skin, until she reacted with a feverish protest, lifting her arms, and locking her fingers behind his neck, her body arching instinctively into the hard heat of his, as her mouth opened to capture the marauding torment of his tongue. The sudden fierce pressure of his mouth, searing into her skin, took Sapphire by surprise, making her realise the extent of Blake's self-control. The kisses he had given her before had been so lightly teasing that she had been lulled into a false sense of security, and yet there was a wild elemental pleasure in responding to Blake's hunger; a knowledge that they were meeting as equals, not child and adult.

When he eventually released her mouth it felt bruised and slightly swollen, and yet the sensation was a pleasurable one, her lips acutely sensitive to the light kisses he caressed them with as he murmured softly, 'Let me take this tee-shirt off, I want to feel you against me, Sapphire.'

His hands were already gripping the edge of her tee-shirt, and to her shame Sapphire knew a wild impulse to help him. Once she had fantasised about seeing their bodies intimately enmeshed; the paleness of her fair skin against the gold-bronze of his and now, treacherously, that memory resurfaced making her protest only a token one as Blake tugged the stretchy fabric up over her body.

Her figure had changed in the intervening years, she knew; her shape no longer that of a young girl. Her waist had narrowed, but her breasts were fuller, more mature, crowned with deep pink nipples, at the moment veiled from Blake's intense scrutiny by the lacy fabric of her bra.

'Beautiful,' he murmured huskily, his thumb stroking caressingly along the edge of the dainty lace and down into the hollow between her breasts.

Desire seemed to explode like fireworks deep inside her, stunning Sapphire with its intensity. She had desired Blake before, but surely never with this consuming, all-important depth, that pushed aside every other emotion as trivial and not to be considered. She wanted to respond to him with every feminine nerve ending; she wanted to feel his hands and mouth against every inch of her skin; and she wanted the freedom to caress and know him in exactly the same way. The knowledge that she could feel like this was shocking and yet exciting; freeing her suddenly from the fear she had always had that somehow she was not quite 100 per cent feminine; that the deep inner core of her was cold and unfunctioning. No other man had made her feel like this, certainly not Alan.

Alan! She tensed, suddenly shocked back to reality. Blake's fingers were curled round the lacy cup of her bra, his eyes so brilliantly gold as he stared down at her that she found herself blinking, half-dazzled by their glitter.

'Blake, I don't want. . .' She shivered as he cut off her protest by bending his head and brushing his lips provocatively along the delicate skin exposed above the white lace.

A tumult of sensations poured moltenly through Sapphire's veins. She made a small sound, meant to be a protest, but which emerged as a soft cry of pleasure as Blake's fingers eased back the lace and his lips followed the path they made until they found the aching centre of her breast, being teased into wanton erectness by the caressing movement of his fingers.

Awash with pleasure Sapphire was barely aware of Blake unsnapping her bra, and exposing her other breast until he repeated his tormenting caresses on it with a nerve-racking delicacy that left Sapphire shivering and aching beneath an onslaught of pleasure she hadn't believed could exist.

'You respond to me as though no-one's ever touched you like that before,' Blake muttered rawly, cupping her breasts possessively as he looked up at her. 'I expected you to be more blasé.'

As she shuddered in reaction, he moaned thickly, 'Don't do that, you make me go up in flames, just thinking about. . .' His sudden tension alerted Sapphire to the sound of a vehicle arriving in the yard.

'Damn,' Blake swore softly. 'The last thing I feel like right now is leaving this bed.'

His words brought Sapphire back down to earth, making her shrink in self-disgust from her own behaviour. How could she have behaved so foolishly? She was lucky that Blake didn't appear to have guessed how much she still cared about him. . . Stunned, Sapphire stopped what she was doing. That wasn't true, she didn't care about Blake at all. . . But if that was true, why had she reacted so intensely to him . . . why had her body welcomed him as its lover? She *didn't* still love him; she *couldn't* . . . but deep inside Sapphire knew that she was only deceiving herself. If sex was really her only motivation she could have found that with anyone of a dozen or more attractive men whom she had dated since leaving Blake, but she hadn't wanted to. She had remained sexually cold to them. She still loved Blake all right, and deep down inside her she must have known it all along, even though she had tried to hide from the truth.

Sick at heart, too numb almost to pull on her tee-shirt, she heard someone knocking on the back door, and hurriedly completed her task.

'I'll get it,' she told Blake, too disturbed to turn and look at him.

The rich smell of their evening meal filled the warm kitchen as Sapphire hurried across it, her hair was uncombed and her face free of makeup, her lips no doubt still swollen from Blake's kisses. A flush of embarrassment stained her skin as she pulled open the door, and then came to an abrupt halt, stunned by the sight of the very last person she had expected to see standing there.

'Alan,' she managed weakly, staring at him, thinking how out of place his dark business suit and obviously new sheepskin jacket looked—and how alien he seemed to her. She had only been away from London for a few days, but already it seemed like another life-time.

'Your father told me you were here,' Alan frowned. 'I've been to make arrangements to get the car back. You really should have been more careful, Sapphire, and what are you doing here?' he demanded waspishly. 'I expected to find you with your father, instead he directed me here ... or rather his housekeeper did. Not a very forthcoming woman, but then I suppose it's only to be expected from these country types. Aren't you going to let me in?' he asked her querulously. 'It's freezing out here, and what on earth are you wearing?' He surveyed her jean-clad figure with open disapproval. 'Sapphire, what's going on, I. . .'

'Why don't you tell him, darling?'

Blake's voice from the other side of the kitchen made Sapphire wrench her head round in open-mouthed disbelief. Clad only in a towelling robe, Blake stood by the door, arms folded, hair tousled, the sight of his bare chest and long lean legs making Sapphire go weak at the knees, treacherous, reactionary sensations warming the pit of her stomach.

'Sapphire, who is this?' Alan demanded.

'Blake,' Blake offered, answering for her, and walking towards Alan, proferring his hand, 'Sapphire's husband.'

'Husband!' Alan practically goggled, and watching him Sapphire knew that no matter how she might have chosen to deceive herself, when it came to it, she would never have married Alan. The emotions she felt for him were lukewarm nonentities when compared with the fierce, tumultuous feelings she had for Blake.

'Yes, Sapphire and I have decided to give our marriage another try,' Blake told him calmly.

'Marriage. You told me you were divorced,' Alan accused Sapphire. 'When did all this happen? Why didn't you say something when I rang?'

'I wanted to tell you, Alan, but. . .'

'I was hoping your father would put me up for the night. It's too late to drive back to London now, and there isn't a decent hotel in miles.'

'You can stay here,' Blake offered, stunning Sapphire with his offer. 'There's plenty of room. If you bring in your case I'll take it upstairs for you—it will give you and Sapphire a chance to talk.'

Sapphire had expected Alan to refuse, but instead he walked out to his hired car and returned with an overnight case. When Blake took it upstairs Alan demanded, 'What's going on? When you left London you were going to marry me, now. . .'

'I'm sorry, Alan, but I didn't want to tell you over the phone. I thought you'd ring again before coming up here, and everything's happened so quickly that. . .'

'By everything I suppose you mean going to bed with your supposed "ex",' Alan interrupted crudely. 'He's obviously got something I don't have. . . . Oh, come on Sapphire,' he added angrily when she tried to protest, 'it's written all over the pair of you. Well I'm beginning to think he's welcome to you. You aren't the woman I thought, that's obvious,' he added in disgust, 'and if it wasn't for necessity, there's no way I'd stay here tonight. My sister was right it seems. She warned me not to get too involved with you.'

Alan's sister was a domineering possessive woman whom Sapphire had never liked and she sighed faintly.

'I've put your case in your room. The door on the right,' Blake announced, coming back into the kitchen. 'How long until we eat?' he asked Sapphire, 'I want to check on the mare and foal. Sapphire told you about her midwifery skills yet?' he asked Alan. 'She's practically delivered him all by herself. Messy business too—breech birth. . .'

Alan had gone green and Sapphire suppressed a momentary flash of irritation against him. Poor Alan, he couldn't help being so squeamish. If she didn't know better she would have thought that Blake was deliberately trying to show him in a bad light. She frowned suddenly, remembering which room Blake had given Alan. That was Blake's own room. Perhaps he had put Alan's case there because he knew the bed was freshly made up, and after all there were plenty of other rooms for him to sleep in.

'We'll be eating in half an hour,' she told him. 'Alan, the bathroom's first on the left if you want to use it.'

CHAPTER SEVEN

IT was definitely one of the worst meals Sapphire had ever endured. Alan had lapsed into a sulky silence, punctuated by petulant little-boy responses to her questions, designed to reinforce her guilt, but what was even harder to cope with was the proprietorial, and very obviously male-in-possession, stance adopted by Blake, who remained sublimely indifferent to the killing looks she gave him, taking every opportunity he could to touch her, or to look at her with such blatant sexuality that if she hadn't known exactly why he was doing it, she would have been in serious danger of succumbing to them.

Afterwards both men accepted coffee, and the tense silence pervading the sitting room as they all sat drinking it made Sapphire heave a sigh of relief when Blake announced that he ought to go and do his final rounds.

'We go to bed early in these parts,' he told Alan blandly.

'Yes, I'm sure with the livestock and. . .'

'Oh that isn't the only reason,' Blake interrupted softly, watching Sapphire.

'I thought you told me you hated him,' Alan said stiffly the moment they were alone, 'and yet now, apparently you're reconciled.'

For a moment Sapphire was tempted to tell him the truth, as she had been planning to, but what was the point now? It was kinder in the long run to let Alan have the pride-saving cleansing of genuine anger to sustain him, and it would be selfish of her to tell him the truth now, knowing that she could never marry him.

'I made a mistake,' she told him quietly.

'But not as big a one as I made,' Alan told her through his teeth. 'I thought . . . oh what's the use? I might as well try and get what sleep I can. I'm leaving here in the morning. I'll have your office cleared out and your things sent on.'

'Thank you.' How stilted and formal they were with one another. Sapphire sighed. She wished they could have remained friends, but sensed that Alan's sister would prevent that!

When she had finished clearing away from their meal Sapphire went upstairs herself. Blake was still outside, and a thin line of light showed under the door of the room he had given Alan, the bathroom door open.

After showering in the privacy of her own en suite bathroom Sapphire towelled herself dry, clicking her tongue impatiently as she realised she had left her nightdress on the bed. Thank heavens for central heating, she reflected self-indulgently, as she dropped her damp towel and walked through into the other room. The lamps on either side of the half tester bed threw a soft haze of peach light across the room, emphasising the subtle blues of the decor, her progress silent as she wriggled her toes luxuriously in the thick blue pile of the carpet.

She was just picking up her nightdress when she froze in disbelief as the handle of her bedroom door turned. Clutching the thin silk to herself she stared as the door opened inwards and Blake walked casually in.

'Blake!' Her astonishment showed in her voice. 'What are you doing in here?'

'I am your husband,' he reminded her tauntingly, 'or is the maidenly shock because you were expecting someone else—your lover, perhaps? Sorry to disappoint you, but unless he wants to share your bed with me as well as with you, he'll have to sleep alone tonight,' Blake told her crudely.

Sapphire was too stunned to be embarrassed about her nudity, anger heating her blood to boiling point as she stared at him. 'Alan would never . . .' she began, only to be interrupted by Blake who drawled insultingly, 'Oh surely that can't be true, Sapphire? He must have wanted you once at least for you to be lovers, but not under my roof, and not while you're wearing my ring, and just to make sure he doesn't, I'll be sleeping in here with you tonight.'

'You can't.' The protest was out before she could stop it, her eyes widening with shock. 'Blake, there are half-a-dozen bedrooms for you to choose from. . .'

'But I've chosen this one,' he told her grimly, adding, 'Oh come on, Sapphire, I wasn't born yesterday, you really didn't think I was going to make it easy for you do you? You alone in one room, him virtually next door? When did you arrange for him to come here?'

He was across the room in four strides, gripping her upper arm with fingers that bit into the soft flesh, surprising a gasp of pain from her lips.

'Blake, I didn't arrange anything. I was as surprised as you to see him. Oh I knew he was coming to collect his car. . .' Anger fired her eyes to deep blue-black as she added bitterly, 'Why should I defend my actions to you? There's no reason why I should be faithful to you, Blake, no reason at all.'

'No?' His face was white with anger. 'Then perhaps I'd better give you one. Why didn't you tell him you were coming back to me, Sapphire? Were you afraid he wouldn't wait for you, is that it?'

'I wanted to tell him in person, not over the telephone. Alan fully understands the situation,' she lied, urged to utter the falsehood by some only dimly conceived knowledge that if Blake thought she still loved Alan, it would in some way protect her from him. This afternoon she had come dangerously close to succumbing to the raw masculinity of him; of succumbing to her own reluctantly admitted love for him, she told herself. If Blake discovered how she really felt she had no guarantee that he wouldn't somehow manipulate her vulnerable emotions and her, using them to his own best advantage. She shivered suddenly, wishing she had not as her shudder drew Blake's attention to her nude body.

In the lamplight her skin glowed pearly cream, her hair curling wildly round her shoulders, still damp from her shower, her face completely free of makeup.

'How many times has he seen you like this?' Blake grated hoarsely. 'How many times have you slept with him? How long have you been lovers?'

'That's none of your business,' Sapphire protested, hot colour flooding her skin. 'I don't ask you about your . . . your love life. . .'

'Love life!' Blake laughed harshly. 'Now there's

an antiquated term if ever there was one. I don't
have a *love life*, my dear wife, I learned the folly of
that years ago, but I do have all the usual sexual
desires. . . Like me to prove it to you?'

'You're disgusting.' Sapphire flung the words at
him as she pulled free of his grip.

'You didn't seem to think so earlier this evening,'
Blake reminded her softly, going back to the
bedroom door where he turned the key in the lock
and then removed it, putting it in his jeans pocket.
'Just in case you have any ideas about going to lover
boy while I'm asleep,' he explained tersely.

What was the matter with Blake? Sapphire
wondered bitterly. He seemed to have a fetish
about her going to Alan. What would he say if he
knew the truth? That Alan wasn't her lover; that
no man ever had been. . . She shuddered; her skin
suddenly too warm, her body weak with the
knowledge that there was only one man she
wanted to make love to her. What would Blake
say if she told him . . . if she asked him. . .

Shocked she pulled her thoughts back from the
precipice on which they teetered. Hadn't she
learned anything at all from the past? Once before
she had begged Blake to love her.

'Don't worry, you're quite safe with me,' Blake
drawled, watching her. 'Unless of course, you
choose not to be.'

'Why on earth should I do that?' Animosity
flared between them; tension tightening Sapphire's
nerve endings.

'Oh any number of reasons,' Blake told her
insultingly. 'You've been up here several days . . .
and it can sometimes be hard denying oneself,
when one's been used to. . .'

'Stop it!' Sapphire demanded, goaded almost beyond endurance, her cheeks scarlet with rage. 'How dare you suggest that. . .'

'That you'd be so hungry for sex that you'd turn to me?' Blake finished coolly for her. 'Why not? After all it wouldn't be the first time, would it?'

He turned his back on her as he spoke, calmly pulling off his sweater and unfastening his shirt, leaving Sapphire seething with temper and pain. How could he throw that in her face? He always had been a cruel bastard, she thought bitterly, but she had never expected anything like this. . .'

'Go on.' His voice was amused rather than contrite. 'Why don't you throw something at me, if that's how you feel.'

'Go to hell,' Sapphire told him thickly. 'God, I hate you, Blake. . .'

'Really?' He paused in the act of unfastening his belt, sitting down on the bed, his eyebrows arching as he studied the warm curves of her body. 'Then perhaps you ought to have a word with your hormones,' he tormented blandly, 'they seem to be getting the wrong message.'

Sapphire had forgotten her nudity, and she froze to the spot, the image of her own body faithfully reflected in the long pier-glass on the other side of the room. Her skin glowed milky pale, her breasts full and softly feminine, crowned with deeply pink nipples that betrayed all too clearly the correctness of Blake's taunt.

'I'm going to have a shower,' Blake told her, standing up and shedding his jeans. Frantically Sapphire dragged her gaze away from the muscled contours of his body, not sure who she hated the most; Blake for tormenting her as he was doing, or herself for being so vulnerable to that torment.

'You can always join me if you want to cool down.' The mocking taunt followed him across the room as he closed the bathroom door behind him. Once he was gone Sapphire struggled into her nightdress. The fine pearl grey silk seemed to emphasise her curves rather than conceal them, the deeply decolleté, lace-trimmed neckline outlining the curves of her breasts in explicit detail. One thing she was sure of. When Blake came back from the bathroom he would find her deeply and safely asleep. As she lay down and pulled the covers over her, keeping as close to the edge of the bed as possible she wondered bitterly if he had come to her room deliberately to torment her, or if he genuinely did believe if he wasn't there to prevent her she might have gone to Alan.

Letting him think that she and Alan were lovers was her only means of protection, she acknowledged, closing her eyes, her body tense. Once Blake found out they weren't, it wouldn't take him long to discover that she still loved him and then she would be completely at his mercy.

Nothing had changed, she thought bitterly, forcing herself to breathe evenly, and then a small inner voice corrected her, one thing had changed apparently. Blake, for some reason, now seemed to find her physically desirable. Or was his desire for her simply a frustrated sexual longing for Miranda who presumably now shared her favours between Blake and her husband? Nausea, deep and wrenching, tore into her as Sapphire pictured them together. No, please God not that, she whispered squeezing her eyes closed as though she could blot out the pictures. She had been through all this once before and suffered all the torments of the damned picturing Blake with Miranda, imagining their bodies entwined in the act of love; sharing its heated ecstasy and its languorous aftermath— pleasures which had been denied to her, and she wasn't going to endure them again. She *couldn't*.

She heard Blake come back into the room and tensed as he snapped off the lamp, and pulled back the covers. The sarcastic comments she had expected about the way she was huddled on the edge of the bed never came, and to her chagrin within minutes of getting into bed, Blake appeared to be fast asleep!

As she struggled up through dense layers of sleep the first thing Sapphire realised was that at some time during the night she must have turned instinctively towards Blake, because now, instead of lying with her back to him, curled up on the edge of the bed she was actually curved against his body, her head pillowed on his shoulder.

Luckily Blake was still asleep and therefore unable to witness her weakness. As she started to move away from him, the second thing Sapphire realised was that he was sleeping nude. Perhaps she ought to have expected it; but during the brief days of their marriage he had always worn pyjamas, the jackets of which he had invariably tugged off at some time during the night, she remembered. Lost in her thoughts; seduced into inert languor by the warmth of his body, she was reluctant to move, even while acknowledging that she should; surely there could be no real harm in indulging herself in these few brief seconds of pleasure. But her conscience prodded her, and unwillingly she started to move away.

'Going somewhere?' Blake's voice, still husky with sleep, rasped tantalisingly against her sensitive skin, making her shiver with a reaction somewhere between delight and dread.

'It's light,' Sapphire told him unnecessarily, trying to edge away from him without drawing his attention to what she was doing, and failing abysmally as he rolled on to his side, pinning her against him with one arm.

He was so close now that she could feel the intimacy of his body heat; the warm, muskily male scent of his skin clouding her reasoning processes, so that it no longer seemed quite so imperative for her to move. Much more pleasant to give in to the allure of remaining where she was.

'I thought you'd want to be out, checking on the stock.' Conscience made her make the feeble concession to saying what she felt she should, but Blake brushed her protest aside.

'The men will be doing that, because I did the last round last night—we're very democratic up here,' he drawled teasingly. 'I must say it was quite a surprise to wake up and find you in my arms. I seem to remember that last night you couldn't get far enough away from me.'

'I didn't know what I was doing,' Sapphire defended herself, 'I must have turned over in my sleep and when. . .'

'You're used to sharing a bed with someone? Like you do with your lover?' Blake accused harshly, 'Is that what you were going to say?'

'And if it was?' Sapphire flung back at him

recklessly. Anything to keep him from discovering just how much she was affected by his proximity.

'Then there must be other things you're missing, beside a warm body in bed beside you at night,' Blake countered softly. Sapphire couldn't tell if it was challenge or anger that turned his eyes to molten gold, but even as she moved away from him, his fingers clamped into her waist, refusing to let her go. As she struggled to free herself her breasts brushed the taut skin of his chest and even through the fabric of her nightdress she was overwhelmingly conscious of the contact, closing her eyes against a sudden too-painful image of skin against flesh, of Blake stroking and caressing her.

'Open your eyes,' Blake demanded harshly, shattering the erotic bubble of her thoughts. 'You aren't going to pretend it's someone else who's holding you in his arms, Sapphire.'

'Who was it who taught you to be so arousingly responsive?' he muttered, his eyes on the swift rise and fall of her breasts, her nipples pressing urgently against the fine fabric of her nightdress, in wanton supplication of the caresses her mind had envisioned so very recently.

Sapphire felt a wave of shame course through her. How could she be behaving in such an abandoned fashion?

'Who?' Blake pressed. 'Your precious Alan, or another lover?'

'Does it matter?' Hot tears stung her eyes, caused as much by his cruel blindness as her own weakness. He was the only man she had ever met who could touch the deep inner core of her femininity; he was the only man with the ability to unleash her desire.

'Perhaps not.' The heat had gone from his voice to be replaced by a cynical blandness. 'That it has been achieved at all is miracle enough I suppose. When I think of the way you used to shy away from me.'

Shy away? Sapphire stared at him. What about all the times she had willed him to make love to her? What about the times she had lain in this bed praying that he would stretch out and touch her?

'I think it's time we were getting dressed,' she told him hurriedly, trying to dispel her tormenting memories.

'So, you haven't changed completely,' Blake drawled. 'You still run away from situations you find unpalatable. Well, this is one occasion my dear wife, when you can't run. Unless, of course you want me to pursue you, and carry you back to this bed?'

'Why should you want to do that?' Sapphire tried to sound sophisticated and amused but instead her voice was a breathy, hesitant whisper Blake's smile telling her that she had not succeeded.

'Do I really have to tell you?' He leaned toward her, the fingers of his free hand curling round the strap of her nightdress and slowly sliding it down her arm. The bedcovers had slipped down to her waist during their earlier struggle, and Sapphire watched like a rabbit transfixed by the hunter as Blake leisurely revealed the creamy slope of her breast.

'You've changed,' he murmured, studying her until the colour ran up under her pale skin 'You're fuller here,' his thumb skimmed the outline of her breast, resting so briefly against her nipple that she couldn't be sure whether the caress was deliberate or accidental, 'and narrower here.'

His fingers touched her waist, and she shivered convulsively, her throat dry and tight with the aching need she could feel burning up inside her. She wanted to slide her fingers into the crisp darkness of his hair, to hold his head against her breast, and caress the male contours of his body. Shame and fear mingled into a stomach-tensing cramp as she tried to fight against her feelings.

'Do you like this?' Blake slid the nightdress free of her breast cupping it with his palm and stroking his tongue along the valley between it and its twin, his thumb making erotic patterns around its rosy peak.

'No.' Her denial was a choked, strangled lie.

'I think you mean yes.' Blake was so lazily self-assured that Sapphire started to tremble. 'Well, Sapphire,' he pressed, 'did you mean yes?' All the time he spoke to her he was teasing, nibbling little kisses closer and closer to her nipple. Heat coursed through her veins. Part of her wanted to flee; to get as far away from him as she could, and the other part wanted to be so close to him that not even the fragile thinness of her nightdress was between them. She ached for the feel of Blake's mouth against her breast; his hands on her body, but as though to punish her for her fib, his kisses stopped tantalisingly short of their goal, and with memories of past rejections to the forefront of her mind Sapphire could not, would not guide his mouth to the place she most wanted it to be.

'Well, then, perhaps you prefer this?'

She was eased out of her nightdress before she had time to object, the embarrassment of Blake's thorough scrutiny of her nude body outweighing all other considerations as she struggled to tug the bedclothes up over her, and Blake effortlessly restrained her. A mocking smile curved his mouth, but it was the showers of gold lightening glittering in his eyes that made Sapphire tense on a sudden spiral of excitement.

His fingertips stroking her hip and then following the line of her body downwards sparked off a showerburst of heady pleasure that she fought to conceal, swallowing the small gasp of delight that threatened to betray how she felt. She badly wanted to touch Blake as freely as he was touching her, to taste the warm maleness of his skin and feel his body come alive beneath her hands.

'You have the loveliest skin.' Blake was still touching her, drawing spiralling patterns against her thigh which transmitted an intensity of heat totally at odds with the lightness of his touch. His voice had a velvet, mesmeric quality that lulled her tense muscles into languorous relaxation. She wanted to purr almost, like a small satisfied cat, Sapphire realised on a stunned wave of surprise; she wanted to stretch and arch beneath those teasing fingers; to prolong the tormenting love play and instigate some of her own.

'Sapphire?'

The sound of her name made her turn her head to look at Blake, her eyes unknowingly a deep dense purple blue.

'Open your mouth,' Blake commanded softly, 'I want to kiss you.'

It was heaven and hell, the zenith of pleasure and the nadir of despair. It was life and death light and dark, and she was no more capable o resisting him than she was of denying that she loved him.

She clung to him, obeying the wordless commands of his mouth, responding with deep, driven intensity of emotion she had not known she could feel, abandoning every last vestige of pride and self-defence as her fingers locked in his hair and she clung with unashamed need to the greater strength of his body.

When at last he released her mouth, he studied its bruised softness for several seconds, his eyes eventually lifting to her bemused eyes, before he kissed her again, this time letting the moist warmth of his lips soothe the sensitive stinging skin of hers.

'You liked that.' It was a statement, not a question, rich with self-satisfaction, the long, lingering look he gave her body that of a man who knows exactly what effect he has had on the woman in his arms. His fingers traced a lazy pattern around and between her breasts, trailing downwards to her waist.

Excitement and urgency arched her body upwards, mutely seeking closer contact with his.

'I think you were right after all. It is time we got dressed.' His words were like snow being trickled down her spine. Sapphire couldn't believe she had heard them. She wanted to protest, to demand to know why he had aroused her so deliberately and turned away from her, but her pride would not allow her to. If Blake could behave as though what had just happened between them meant nothing to him; if he was completely unaffected by the explosion of love and need which had gripped her, then so was she.

CHAPTER EIGHT

SAPPHIRE deliberately dawdled getting dressed, not wanting to face Blake. As she had hoped, when she walked into the kitchen half an hour later there was no sign of him, but the sight of Alan sitting morosely at the table, a mug of coffee in front of him brought her to an abrupt halt.

'So you "hate" him do you?' he sneered bitterly. 'Some way you have of showing it! And to think I held off taking you to bed because I didn't want to stampede you! Oh, it's all right, Sapphire,' he grimaced, the anger deserting him, as he raked tired fingers through his hair. 'He's told me all about it; how the two of you decided to give your marriage another try. I just wish I heard it first from you that's all.'

'I'm sorry, Alan.' Shakily Sapphire sat down, knowing that Alan had every right to feel angry and resentful. 'I didn't tell you over the phone because ... because I didn't think it was the right thing to do. I didn't realise that Blake intended us to be re-married quite so soon.'

'You're happy with him?' His voice was abrupt, tight with a pain that made Sapphire's heart ache in sympathy.

'I do love him,' she told him, avoiding the question.

'And obviously sexually you're extremely compatible,' Alan shocked her by saying. 'Come on, Sapphire, I'm not a complete fool,' he told her

134

roughly, 'when a man comes down for breakfast, looking like a well-fed predator, it isn't hard to guess what's put the smile on his face.'

She wanted to protest that he was wrong, but sensibly did not. Perhaps it might make it easier for Alan to accept the situation if he believed that she and Blake were lovers. Sadly she knew that their friendship was now over, and that once she and Blake had parted there could be no going back to Alan. She would miss him as one always missed good friends, but she did not love him, she acknowledged, her feelings from him came nowhere near to those she felt for Blake.

After he had breakfast Alan insisted on leaving. When he had gone Sapphire felt restless. On impulse she decided to go out for a walk, glimpsing Blake working in one of the snow-covered fields—just a small dark figure by a Land Rover, with something familiar in his stance that tugged at her heart.

Shivering in the cold wind she walked back to the house, still too restless to settle. She would go and see her father; she decided visiting him might help to keep her mind off her own problems.

Flaws farmyard was deserted when she drove in. Someone had cleared the worst of the snow away, and although the kitchen was redolent with the yeasty smell of baking there was no sign of Mary.

Terror, sharp and paralysing, gripped her for a second, a dreadful vision of her father, motionless, dying, rising up before her. The vision cleared and she hurried upstairs, her heart thumping; her pulses racing in aching fear as she pushed open the door to her father's room and came to a full stop.

Far from lying close to death's door on his bed

her father was standing by the window, dressed in a pair of disreputable old trousers and a thick woollen jumper. He looked thinner than Sapphire remembered, but otherwise he was still very much the father of her late teens, his weatherbeaten face turned towards the window, his eyes on the distant snow-covered line of hills.

'Back already,' he commented without looking round. 'I'll just have a cup of coffee Mary and then. . .' He turned and saw Sapphire, shock and something else she couldn't understand leaping to life in his eyes.

'Sapphire!'

The room started to tilt and spin and Sapphire heard a roaring sound in her ears, increasing in volume until it drowned out everything else. Dimly she was aware of her father calling for Mary, of blackness coming down over her, and then a thick, suffocating darkness that seemed to press down all around her.

When she opened her eyes she was sitting in her father's chair, Mary standing anxiously at her side.

'My, you gave us all a shock fainting like that,' she told Sapphire worriedly. 'Are you all right now?'

'Dad . . .' Sapphire croaked unevenly, 'when I came in and everywhere was so quiet, I thought. . .'

Shock, and something else she couldn't name shadowed Mary's eyes. She was about to speak when the door opened and her father walked in. *Walked in*, Sapphire noted dazedly, carrying a mug of tea.

'Come on, drink this,' Mary instructed her. 'It

will help allay the shock.' The 'phone started to ring and as Sapphire took the mug from her father Mary said briskly, 'I'd better go down and answer that.'

When she had gone Sapphire looked at her father. 'Sorry about this,' she apologised huskily, 'but you gave me such a shock. . .'

'Aye, I'm sorry too, lass.' Her father looked sad and disturbed. 'I thought. . .' He shook his head. 'No, we won't talk about it now, Sapphire. You're in no fit state. You stay here and rest for a while and I'll. . .'

He broke off as Mary came in her round face creased into a thoughtful frown.

'That was Blake,' she told them both. 'In a rare old state, wanting to know if we'd seen anything of you.' She looked at Sapphire and smiled. 'That must have been some spat the two of you had to generate so much concern, and the pair of you not a week reconciled yet.'

Knowing that her father was watching her Sapphire summoned a light smile. 'Blake wasn't too pleased when Alan turned up last night,' she told them, hoping she would be forgiven her small fib, but not wanting to let them guess at the real state of affairs between herself and Blake.

'Jealous, was he?' her father laughed. 'Aye well, I suppose it's my fault for sending the laddie over to you, but I thought it best.'

'He's gone now,' Sapphire told them, and explained briefly.

'I'd better get back,' she told her father. She couldn't put off facing Blake for ever. From somewhere she would have to find the determination to remind him that their marriage was a strictly platonic one. Not that he could really want her, she reminded herself bitterly.

'You stay right here,' Mary scolded her. 'You're in no fit state to be driving after that faint. Blake's coming to take you home. He's getting one of the men to drive him over in the Land Rover. He'll be here in ten minutes or so.'

Shakily Sapphire drank her tea. Why had Blake rung Flaws Farm? Had he perhaps gone back to the house this morning and wondered where she was? She frowned, and then tensed as she heard the familiar sound of a Land Rover engine.

'Here he is now,' Mary announced going to look out of the window. 'I'll go down and tell him where we are. No, don't you get up,' she told Sapphire sternly. 'I'm not too happy about that faint of yours. You must try and take things easy for a few days. Put on a few pounds, perhaps. I know it's fashionable to be slim but you seem to have been overdoing things.'

'Now she's back with Blake, she'll soon fatten up a bit,' her father prophesied. 'There's nothing like a happy marriage.'

Sighing Sapphire turned her face away. What would her father say if he knew the truth? But he mustn't know the truth, she thought in panic. She could already see the effect their re-marriage had had on his health; he was marvellously improved. It couldn't last for long of course, but she daren't take the risk of him discovering the truth.

She heard Mary go downstairs and then return several minutes later accompanied by Blake. Where earlier she had been shocked to see how much healthier her father had appeared than she had anticipated, now she was equally startled by the pallor of Blake's skin and the tense, bitter, brooding darkness of his eyes.

'Mary tells me you fainted.' His voice was almost accusatory.

'It was just the shock of finding Dad out of bed,' she told him knowing how feeble her explanation sounded, but not able to tell him in front of her father of her fears when she had entered the strangely silent house.

She started to get out of the chair, but Blake forestalled her, striding over and bending to pick her up, ignoring her protests.

'Let him carry you,' Mary placated. 'I don't want you falling down those steep stairs. No, she's perfectly all right,' she told Blake who had turned to question her, 'she just needs to rest a little and get her strength back.'

When he had installed her in the passenger seat of his car Blake started the engine, his face grim as he drove the car out of the cobbled yard.

'What did you want me for?' Sapphire ventured once they were out on the road. 'You rang Mary to find out if I was there,' she pressed when he turned to frown at her. 'You must have wanted me for something. . .'

'When I went back to the house and found you missing,' Blake told her harshly, 'it struck me that you might have decided to renege on our bargain.'

It took several seconds for the words to sink in. 'You mean you thought I had left with Alan?' Sapphire said incredulously, 'But. . .'

'But he wouldn't take you, believing that you and I are lovers?' There was a cynically bitter twist to Blake's mouth, his eyes as hard and cold as the snow-encrusted stone walls they were driving past.

'No! I. . .' Oh, what was the use trying to get through to him when he was in this sort of mood, Sapphire thought despairingly. Reaction from her faint had started to set in. She felt sick and tense; in no condition to cope with Blake's biting sarcasm. This was the Blake she remembered, she thought miserably; this hard, cynical man who seemed to be driven by demons she could not comprehend; who seemed to take pleasure in humiliating her.

The moment the car stopped outside the backdoor, she reached for her seatbelt, but Blake was too quick for her, moving swiftly round to her door, and lifting her out of her seat, even as she protested that she could manage.

'What made you faint, Sapphire?' he demanded as he carried her upstairs to their room. 'No wonder you put up so little fight when I suggested we re-marry. But you weren't completely truthful with me were you? What happened? Wouldn't he marry you when he knew that you were carrying his child?'

She was too stunned to answer him. He dropped her unceremoniously on the bed, where she simply lay, staring at him.

'Oh, I confess you had me nicely fooled,' Blake said bitterly. 'It never occurred to me that you. . . We can hardly have our marriage annulled now,' he continued sardonically, 'and that being the case. . .'

He walked back to the bedroom door, calmly locking it and pocketing the key while Sapphire watched him in stupid disbelief. Blake couldn't really believe that she was carrying Alan's child, could he? If that had been the case she would never have consented to this ridiculous re-marriage. Alan would have married her and willingly. Anger swept aside pain. How dare he accuse her of behaving so selfishly? She opened her mouth to tell him the truth and then closed it, her eyes rounding in surprise as he stripped off his sweater and shirt. His hands were on the buckle of his belt before Sapphire realised what was happening, her voice croaky and unsteady as she whispered, 'Blake, just what do you think you're doing?'

'If you're going to foist the responsibility for this child off on me, I might as well have some of the pleasure of fathering it,' he snarled furiously at her. 'It might not be my child, Sapphire, but you are my wife, and since it looks like this time I'm stuck with you, I might as well get whatever I can get out of it. . .'

'I thought all you wanted was my father's land,' Sapphire gritted back at him. 'I won't make love with you, Blake,' she warned him. 'I. . .' Her breath was trapped in her throat as he stepped out of his jeans, flinging them on to the floor. Clad only in dark briefs his body was that of a man used to an active life. Unwillingly Sapphire felt her glance slide helplessly over his broad shoulders, and down across the width of his chest. Dark hair arrowed downwards across the flat tautness of his stomach, and a mad desire to reach out and trace its erotic path rose up inside her. Quelling it, she tore her gaze away, shaken by the force of her reaction.

Two strides brought Blake to the edge of the bed. Leaning down he grasped the lapels of the cotton blouse she was wearing and Sapphire

tensed, blue eyes meeting gold. Her breath stifled
in her throat as Blake's fingers curled into the
fabric, the glitter in his eyes one of dark menace
as he jerked forcefully at the cotton. Buttons
flew in all directions as the blouse tore, unable
to withstand the violence he was doing it.
Sapphire knew she ought to have felt fear; terror
even, but what she did feel was a wild surging
excitement; a primaeval emotion that seemed to
spring from her innermost being and burst into
life, fuelled by the dark determination she could
read in Blake's eyes.

He found the waistband of her denim skirt,
unsnapping it and sliding down the zip. She tried
to push him away, tensing as she heard the almost
feral snarl of anger he gave as he removed her
clutching fingers, and tossed aside her skirt.

Wearing only her bra and briefs she stared up at
him as he loomed over her, willing her body not to
communicate to his her unwilling arousal. Despite
the rage she could feel emanating from him, she
couldn't forget that this was the man she loved;
and that the mere sight of his body was enough to
bring leaping pulses to life inside her, fuelling a
burning ache that instinct told her only his
possession could assuage. She remembered how he
had deliberately aroused her only that morning
and her eyes darkened unknowingly, her tongue
touching the dry outline of her lips. Above her
Blake growled menacingly, and her eyes met his,
reading the eternal message of rage and desire that
glinted there.

'Thinking about him, were you? Pity you fainted
so unpropitiously this morning,' he taunted,
'otherwise I'd never have suspected you could be

pregnant. Despite it all you still have a look of . . . almost innocence about you.'

His eyes darkened over the last few words, almost as though they caused him pain, and mingled with her own resentment that he could so easily think so little of her Sapphire felt a thread of aching response. She wanted to be in his arms, she acknowledged wistfully; she wanted the warm heat of his body against hers; his hands caressing her, his lips. . . A shudder seemed to tear through her, visible in the brief convulsion of her body, escaping in a faint sigh that was lost as Blake gripped her hair, tangling his fingers in it, forcing her face up so that he could look into her eyes as he muttered thickly, 'Forget him,' and then bent to silence her protest with the fierce possession of his mouth.

This was no tentative, explorative kiss, but an explosion of raw emotions, too strong to be confined in neat pigeonholes labelled 'anger' or 'desire', but instinctively Sapphire recognised and responded to them, unaware that her fingers were digging into the muscled smoothness of his shoulder, until Blake released her abruptly.

'No wonder he wanted you,' he told her hoarsely, his fingers stroking lightly down her shoulder and then erotically over the taut outline of her breast, his warm breath fanning her bruised lips. 'If you always react like that I'm only surprised that he didn't want to keep you—or was it the thought of the child that put him off? Is that why you were so quick to accept my offer, Sapphire? Because you knew he didn't want to marry you?'

Anger flared hotly inside her. 'You already seem

to know all the answers, Blake,' she responded brittly, 'so why ask the questions?'

'Perhaps because I'm hoping I don't.' His thumb was rubbing lightly over the thin silk covering her nipple and Sapphire squirmed slightly beneath the tormenting caress, trying to clamp down on the feelings he was arousing inside her.

'What's the matter? Doesn't my touch appeal to you as much as his? I can make you want me, Sapphire.'

'No!' Her denial was meant as a plea for him not to carry out his threat, but Blake chose to ignore it.

'You think not?' he muttered into her throat, searching for and finding the fast-beating pulse that gave the lie to her denial. She could smell the warm musky scent of his body—inflaming her own with a subtle sexual chemistry that made her languorous and weak. The rough hair on his chest rubbed abrasively against her skin as he moved, biting delicately into her skin, making her shiver almost deliriously with pleasure. The fine silk of her bra and briefs was a barrier between them that tormented her, denying her the intimate contact of skin against skin that she now craved and when Blake's hands slid round her back to remove her bra she expelled her breath in a pent-up sigh of relief he couldn't fail to understand. Soft colour filmed her cheeks as he looked down at her, his smile tormentingly cruel.

'Still expect me to believe you don't want me, Sapphire?'

What could she say? That he had misunderstood her initial remark? She turned her head aside, not wanting him to see the betraying sheen of tears she knew wasn't far away and then gasped out loud as she felt the stinging nip of his teeth against the swollen curve of her breast. Hard on the heels on the initial burst of pain came a pleasure so intense that her eyes widened in acknowledgment of it.

'Don't expect me to believe you haven't been touched like that before,' Blake told her thickly, watching her, 'or like this.'

Ripples of pleasure spread shiveringly through her body as his tongue stroked and teased the aching fullness of her breasts, making her tense and arch in a mindless frenzy of need she hadn't known herself capable of feeling. She dimly heard Blake's suddenly harsh breathing in counterpoint to her own quick shallow breaths, and then his hands slid to her waist, gripping its slenderness until his mouth opened over first one nipple and then the other, tasting, sucking, tugging, while Sapphire felt she would explode with the intensity of pleasure building up inside her.

Unable to stop herself, she moaned Blake's name, reaching up to stroke the hard contours of his back with hands suddenly desperately eager for the feel of his skin against them, scattering wild, impassioned kisses over his shoulder, using her teeth to deliver delicate little nips that drew a hoarse groan of satisfaction from his throat.

All sense of restraint and commonsense abandoned, Sapphire didn't allow herself to think or reason. This was Blake who she still loved as desperately now as she had done when they first married; and if he had accused her so unfairly, well what did it matter now that she was in his arms and he was touching and kissing her with a hunger that her body recognised even if her mind could not. It was a hunger that fed and matched her own, his body whispering to hers that it too had starved and ached for this tumultuous pleasure they were now sharing. Despite the fact that they had never before made love, there was nothing tentative or exploratory in their embraces. Sapphire responded to the intimacy of Blake's touch as intuitively as though they had been lovers for years. Her lips brushed the flat hardness of his nipple and she registered the surprised shock of pleasure jolting through him. His eyes closed, his mouth warm against the indentation of her waist, as she lay half-pinned beneath him, indolently admiring the sculptured perfection of his body.

She ran her fingers lightly down the dark arrowing of hair, stopping when she reached his briefs. He tensed, and then demanded thickly, 'Touch me, Sapphire.'

She let her fingers stray exploratively over the thin cotton of his briefs, her touch slightly hesitant and unsure, her heart thudding violently in response to the small, liquid sound of pleasure emerging from Blake's throat. Heated, muttered words of praise and encouragement overwhelmed all her shyness and reserve. When Blake tugged off his briefs her breath caught in her throat, her eyes unknowingly widening slightly.

'A man could be in danger of forgetting that he's only mortal under a look like that,' Blake told her throatily, sliding his hand round her throat, his thumb under her chin tilting her face up to meet his.

Passion blazed into life as they kissed, her mouth opening willingly to admit the penetration of his tongue, seeking, taking all the warm sweetness she gave up so willingly.

Blake's free hand was resting possessively against her thigh, a heavy warm weight that tantalised and excited her, her own fingers stroking and cajoling the strong muscles of his back, sliding round to investigate the sharp angles of his hips, moving in restless, roving urgency as she responded to the hunger in Blake's kiss.

He released her to tease a chain of moist caresses in a line that investigated the valley between her breast and the slight swell of her stomach.

The restless urgency in the pit of her stomach increased and in obedience to its commands Sapphire brushed her own lips against the firmness of Blake's belly, thrilling to the sudden tension in muscles finely tuned to her light touch. His skin tasted warm and slightly salty, its flavour almost addictive. Lost in the veil of pleasure touching him had revealed to her, she let her lips travel where they wished barely aware of Blake's harsh groan of protest until he snatched her up, rolling her beneath the constraining weight of his body, parting her legs with his thigh, muttering her name like a litany as his fingers touched her intimately, making her yield and ache for his possession.

Far beyond remembering the accusation that had preceded their lovemaking, Sapphire wasn't ready for the unexpected burst of pain. Her muscles tensed immediately, shock mingling with hurt as she fought to understand the too-swift transition from pleasure to pain.

Above her she heard Blake curse, a fiercely bitter sound, his body withdrawing from hers.

Suddenly the pain was gone, and shamelessly she clung to him, refusing to let him go, her eyes pleading mutely with him as her fingers dug into his shoulders, her soft, 'Blake, please . . .' dragging an anguished mutter of response from his throat as he tensed and then shuddered and her body melted in welcome to his, her senses singing with pleasure.

Never had pleasure seemed so tangible, her body was awash with it, glowing, so supremely fulfilled that she wanted to tell the whole world. Stretching indolently she turned her head. Blake was lying inches away, his eyes open, his expression sombre. Of course, this wasn't the first time he had experienced such feelings—not by a long way.

'There's never been anyone else, has there?' he asked the question in a flat voice that drained her pleasure as effectively as a tap being turned on. Sapphire shook her head.

'Then for God's sake why didn't you say so?'

No need to ask if he was regretting making love to her. It was there, written all over his face, etching into his scathing voice.

'I didn't think you'd listen.' She turned away from him, not wanting him to see how vulnerable she was. Neither of them had mentioned love . . . but silently in her heart she had told him how she felt about him, just as her body told his how much it worshipped and adored him.

'So you decided to let me find out for myself?'

'I didn't think I could have stopped you.'

'Half-a-dozen words or so would have done it— "I'm still a virgin", for instance.'

Sapphire arched her eyebrows, turning back to

face him. 'And you'd have believed me?' She turned away again. 'I'd better get dressed. . .'

'No.' Blake's voice was sharp. He swung himself out of bed. 'No, stay here and rest for a while, I'll go down and make you a drink.'

'I'm not an invalid, Blake,' she protested, flushing as his eyes studied her pale skin and slender body. Still bathed in the warm afterglow of their lovemaking she hadn't bothered to cover herself, but now she felt a need to do so, chilled by the way Blake was studying her. Was he comparing her to Miranda? She felt sick at the thought.

'You're not exactly in the peak of *health* either,' he told her still watching her. There was a dark, brooding quality to his look that saddened her. Was he already regretting what had happened?

She reached out towards him, her eyes unconsciously pleading, 'Blake, I. . .'

'Stay here and rest.' He had his back to her and was already getting dressed. Feeling dejected, Sapphire huddled beneath the bed-clothes. Plainly Blake didn't want to talk to her. She closed her eyes, knowing she should regret what had happened but knowing that she did not. Where was her pride? When Blake left the easy, weak tears of physical release flowed for a few seconds and then stopped. By the time he came back with her tea Sapphire was fast asleep. He stood watching her for several seconds with shuttered eyes, before turning to leave, his face grim.

CHAPTER NINE

'SAPPHIRE, we have to talk.'

They were sitting in front of the log fire she had lit just before dinner. Blake had suggested they have their coffee there and now she tensed dreading what he might be about to say. She had been awaiting this moment with mingled apprehension and anguish ever since she had woken up this afternoon. Had Blake guessed that she still loved him? Was he going to tell her that what had happened between them had been caused by some mental aberration. That he would never have made love to her had he been in his right senses? Was he going to tell her about Miranda?

She risked a glance at him. He was sitting opposite her on a chair, his upper body leaning forward, elbows braced on his thighs as he dropped his head into his hands and pushed weary fingers through his hair.

A wave of love overwhelmed her. She wanted to reach out and touch him; to wipe away the lines of exhaustion fanning out from his eyes; to touch and caress him, to. . .

'Sapphire!' The tone of his voice warned her that he knew her thoughts were wandering, his fingers steepled together as he watched her over them, the liquid gold of his eyes dulled, their expression almost stark.

'I never intended what happened this afternoon to take place,' he began abruptly, causing a thousand sharp knives to tear jaggedly at Sapphire's aching heart.

'I know that,' she interrupted curtly. 'I do have a memory, Blake, I'm well aware of the fact that you don't find me desirable. When we first married. . .'

'Don't be ridiculous, of course I find you desirable.' Angry fingers raked through his hair again. 'Hell, Sapphire,' he growled impatiently, 'you're not *that* innocent. If I don't desire you what the hell do you think that was all about this afternoon?'

Colour flamed momentarily in her face as she recalled the fierce intensity of their lovemaking; the feeling she had had at the time that both of them were suffering from the same driven compulsion; the same starving hunger. Quickly she reminded herself of the past, of the early days of their marriage. 'You may desire me now, Blake, but when we were first married, you couldn't bear to touch me; you. . .'

'I don't want to talk about the past.' His voice was clipped and brusque, defying her to continue the subject. 'We're living in the present now, Sapphire, and despite everything wc said before we re-married, it must be as obvious to you now, as it is to me, that we can't live together platonically.'

Her muscles seemed to be seized in a paralysing grip, her body totally unable to function, and then as the great wave of pain crashed down over her Sapphire knew her immobility was simply a defensive measure; a way of stopping the pain, only it had failed miserably. It seemed to fill every corner of her, drowning out pride and reserve. She wanted to cry out to Blake not to send her away;

she wanted to plead with him to stay with her, but instead she remained unspeaking, dreading opening her mouth in case she voiced her anguished thoughts.

'Well?'

Blake was plainly waiting for a response, and when she didn't make one, said tersely, 'Come on, Sapphire, I know you . . . you were a virgin—and that fact alone merely reinforces what I feel—but you must know that sexually we're extremely compatible, almost explosively so,' he muttered half under his breath.

His words were so totally at variance to what she had expected to hear that Sapphire simply stared at him. 'Come on,' Blake demanded half-aggressively, 'Admit it Sapphire, when I made love to you, you enjoyed it. You. . .'

'Yes.' Her simple admission seemed to rob him of breath. 'I did enjoy it, Blake.'

Colour lay dark red along the ridge of his cheekbones, his eyes the flaming gold she remembered from that afternoon, their gaze trained on her, tracking every betraying expression that crossed her face. He breathed deeply, exhaling slowly, his chest rising and falling with the effort.

'Why were you still a virgin?' He was looking directly at her, and Sapphire knew an insane desire to laugh. Pure nerves she told herself, taking a deep breath of her own to steady her.

'At first when I left here I felt too bruised mentally to even think of loving anyone. Later . . .' she shrugged, 'Well, there just wasn't anyone I wanted, and then I met Alan. . .'

She paused, telling herself that it wasn't really

lying to tell him the truth as she had believed it to be before realising that she still loved him. He didn't want her love, and if he knew how she felt he could easily send her away, when, in reality, all she wanted to do was to stay.

Ignoring the inner warning voices that told her she was courting even greater unhappiness than she had already experienced, she continued softly, '. . . I wanted to be sure that what we felt for one another was right. Alan felt the same way. Before I came up here we were planning to go away together for a holiday. We were going. . .'

'To be lovers? In some romantic, idyllic setting?' Blake demanded harshly. 'Mentally you were ready to make love, and because your boyfriend wasn't available you substituted me, is that what you're trying to tell me?' He looked so murderously angry that Sapphire knew a frisson of fear.

'Perhaps, subconsciously,' she lied bravely— anything rather than risk him guessing the truth. 'But no, I didn't consciously substitute you for Alan, Blake.'

'And am I also supposed to believe that we were good together because you thought I was someone else?'

Slowly Sapphire shook her head. She daren't risk trying to pretend that. Blake was angry enough already. Obviously she had touched some nerve of touchy male pride which it would be unwise to press on too hard. 'You're the one with the experience—not me,' she reminded him simply. 'Personally I don't think it would be possible to deceive oneself to that extent, but. . .'

'It isn't.' Blake's voice was so harsh, his face so shuttered and forbidding that she wondered what personal anguish lay behind the curt words, but could not bring herself to ask.

'So,' he told her, 'given that sexually we both agree that we're extremely compatible, I submit that we change the rules of our partnership.'

'Change the rules?' Sapphire was so surprised that she could only repeat what he had said, staring uncomprehendingly up at him. For an instant there was something in his eyes that warmed the ice-coldness of her heart, but it was gone almost immediately his voice crisp and businesslike as he said firmly. 'Yes. We agreed that our relationship would be a platonic one lasting just as long as. . .'

'My father lives,' Sapphire finished for him, her face white. For a few hours she had forgotten her father's condition. Mentally castigating herself she tried to concentrate on what Blake was saying. 'Now I'm suggesting that we lift that self-imposed ban; that we make our marriage a real one in every sense of the word, to be. . .'

'Set aside when we no longer desire one another?'

'Is that what you want?'

His eyes narrowed as he waited for her response, and Sapphire felt a quiver of apprehension deep down inside her. Had he guessed how she felt? It was pride and pride alone that kept her from crying out that she wanted to be with him for ever; that she wanted to share his life and his bed for just as long as her life lasted. Instead she said lightly, 'Yes, of course.'

A mask seemed to drop down over his features, his eyelids lowering to conceal his thoughts from her. 'Very well then,' he said at last. 'If those are your terms, then for as long as our desire lasts, so does our marriage.' He stood up, stretching lithely, and completely changing the subject said calmly, 'Snow's melting. I'll just go out and check on the foal. Why don't you have an early night? You still look washed out.'

Very flattering, Sapphire thought wrathfully ten minutes later, luxuriating in a deep scented bath of deliciously hot water. She wasn't going to question Blake's abrupt volte-face, nor his suggestion that their marriage continue. Perhaps he was hoping to quench his desire for Miranda with her. Perhaps the fact that Miranda was now married broke Blake's own personal code of behaviour, Sapphire didn't know.

One half of her urged flight and safety, reminding her of all the pain he had already caused her, while the other whispered that life without him had been arid, dead; and that perhaps his desire for her could flower into something stronger and more permanent if it was carefully nurtured and protected.

She lingered so long in the bath, deep in thought, that the water started to cool. A draught from the door as it opened made her shiver and she turned round thinking it must have swung open.

'You've been in here so long I was beginning to wonder if my suggestion was so offensive to you that you'd decided you preferred a watery grave to another night in my arms.'

The sight of Blake standing beside the bath, looking down at her, was so unexpected and startling that she could barely breathe. 'I was thinking,' she told him huskily, shivering again as her skin chilled. 'I'm sorry if you've been waiting for the bathroom.' How formal her voice sounded, her expression hunted as she looked past him to where she had left her towel, trying not to think about the hunger that had started to unfurl inside her at the thought of 'a night in his arms'.

'It's large enough for us to share,' Blake drawled reaching for his electric razor, and wiping some of the steam off the mirror above the basin as he plugged it in and switched it on.

'Blake, it's cold in here...' He was halfway through shaving when she finally plucked up the courage to remind him, albeit obliquely, that she wanted to get out of the bath. He finished what he was doing, rubbing his jaw experimentally. 'I thought you always shaved in the morning,' Sapphire muttered crossly. Why couldn't he take the hint and leave her in privacy to get ready for bed?

'So I did,' he agreed blandly, unplugging the razor and turning round to lean indolently against the wall, watching her, 'but married men, my sweet, always shave at night. It saves wear and tear on delicate feminine skin,' he pointed out, grinning openly when she started to blush. The colour seemed to start at her toes and wash up over her body until it reached the swell of her breasts, now barely concealed by the cold bubbles, 'and if you're cold, why don't you get out of the bath?' He saw her tense and instinctively try to submerge more of her body beneath the bubbles and leant towards her. 'Why so shy? You weren't this afternoon.'

How could she explain that that had been different; that then in the heat of passion her own nudity had not disturbed her, but that now in the small confines of the bathroom, with Blake still fully dressed, it did?

All she could manage was a cross, 'You seem to forget that unlike you, I'm not used to . . . to. . .'

'Living with someone? The only person I've ever lived with is you, Sapphire.' As he spoke he was unfastening his shirt buttons. When he had finished he tugged it off, revealing the tautly muscled expanse of his chest. Her breath seemed to lock inside her as Sapphire tried to drag her hungry gaze away from his body.

'Since you won't get out of your own volition, and since I'm too much of a gentleman to let you freeze, I'll just have to help you, won't I?' Blake drawled, and as he leaned towards her, Sapphire realised why he had removed his shirt, and tried automatically to evade him. The small tidal wave her hurried movements caused soaked Blake's jeans, but didn't prevent him from lifting her out of the bath. His chest felt warm and hard against her water-chilled damp flesh, a shivering that had nothing to do with the cold raising goose bumps over her sensitised skin.

'Blake!' Her half-shocked protest was ignored. 'You're soaking wet,' she pointed out breathlessly, trying to clamp down on her rising excitement and totally unable to do so. This close she could see the pores in his skin, the mingled scent of sweat and heat coming off it provocatively arousing.

'We both are,' he agreed, slowly letting her slide to the floor, while reaching for her towel with his free hand, 'but it can soon be remedied.' His eyes never left her face as he enveloped her in the large soft towel and then slowly started to rub her dry.

Within seconds of his touching her Sapphire had forgotten how chilled she had been. Her body seemed to be bathed with heat, consumed by it everywhere he touched her. She had never dreamed that something as mundane as drying her damp skin could be so unbelievably erotic but the gentle friction of the towel against her skin, in Blake's hands became an instrument of exquisite pleasure that delighted and yet intruded unbearably, stopping her from savouring the touch of Blake's hands against her skin—a touch she now burned and hungered for even more than she had this afternoon. He only had to touch her and she went up in flames, she realised shudderingly, almost lightheaded with desire.

'Blake.' His name was a muffled protest and a plea, lost against his chest as she gave in to an overwhelming urge to reach out and touch him, pressing trembling lips to the hard column of his throat, and glorying in his responsive shudder.

'Tell me you want me.' The hoarse command was one she couldn't resist.

'I want you.'

The towel fell away as he picked her up and strode through into the bedroom. Against her body she could feel the fierce thud of Blake's heart, pounding out an unmistakably erotic message, his body, hard and urgent as he deposited her on the bed, tugging off his wet jeans before joining her.

'Show me how much,' he demanded thickly, tracing an erotic pathway downwards along her throat, his fingers burning fiery brands of possession against her skin as he cupped the silky skin of her breast, delicately stroking the hard nub of her nipple. This time Sapphire responded immediately without hesitation, knowing with one corner of her mind that mingled with her desire and love was a tiny thread of desperation urging her to take as much of him as she could while she could—memories to store up to keep her warm on those nights when her bed would be cold and empty without him. As though her yearning hunger reached out and unleashed some deep core of need within him Blake reacted to her passion, touching her, kissing her with a barely restrained ferocity that left her weakly clinging to him like a drowning person to a raft. His touch, his need, the words of passion and hunger he muttered into her ear, took her far beyond the shores of love and out into an ocean so deep she knew that without him she would sink and never ever re-surface.

Fierce tremors of pleasure raced through her body, each lingering caress making her arch and invite with a sensuality that left one corner of her mind half-shocked. Could this really be her, touching Blake with a far greater intimacy than she had ever envisaged; stroking and kissing the taut male body until Blake cried out in a delirium of need, reaching for her, taking the fullness of one breast deeply into his mouth and laving it with the moist heat of his tongue.

Now it was her turn to cry out with pleasure and to experience the fierce shudder of pleasure slamming through Blake's body as he responded to that cry. His fingers stroked circles of fire along the inside of her thigh her body aching with the intensity of her need. He touched her intimately and she melted, twisting and turning, breathing in short, muffled gasps.

'It's no good, I can't wait any longer.' Blake's groaned admission echoed her own thoughts, her body wildly exulting in his swift possession and frenziedly responding to it. The world seemed to explode around them Sapphire crying out with pleasure at each powerful thrust of his body, her nails scoring heatedly along his back as she sought to prolong the contact her body craved even after the climax had been reached and the deep ache inside her soothed.

She felt Blake move away slightly and murmured an incoherent protest. 'Hush. . .' His mouth covered hers briefly, warm and moist and she was shocked to feel the light spiral of desire twist through her so quickly after she thought it had been sated. She tried to move away when Blake bent his head to suck lightly on her swollen and slightly sore nipples, but the pleasure of his touch seduced her into staying where she was, dreamily contemplating the smooth warmth of his skin, reaching out lazy fingers to stroke idly along the ridge of his shoulder.

When his lips grazed across her stomach she felt too indolent to protest, simply looking down at the thick darkness of his hair and wondering awedly that one person could be so vitally important to her happiness.

Blake's fingers touched her thigh, and she tensed as his tongue touched her so intimately that she almost recoiled from the shock of it, trying to pull away and yet at the same time consumed by the molten heat his intimacy engendered until she was giving herself up to it, abandoning herself completely to the sensual spell he was weaving around her, unaware that she was crying out his name.

This time their coming together was less tumultuous, more leisurely and prolonged; Blake's fierce cry of exultation muffled by her kiss, her arms holding him locked against her body as she savoured the sweet aftermath of their pleasure. She fell asleep still holding him, waking during the night to discover that their positions were reversed and that he was now the one holding her, the heavy weight of one leg thrown across her body, pinning her close against him. Sleepily content she nestled closer to him gloating over the pleasure of being able to do so; of being free to reach out and touch the matted hair on his chest; to place her lips to the pulse thudding slowly in his throat. Maybe he only wanted her, but she loved him and hopefully, God willing, they could yet build a relationship; a marriage that could last.

She fell asleep on that thought waking to find herself alone. Downstairs in the kitchen she found a note propped up against the teapot and a small smile tugged at her lips as she read it.

'Market Day,' Blake had written. 'Don't expect me back until late—suggest you catch up on your sleep!'

She spent the morning in a blissful daze, knowing that she was walking around with a smile on her face like a cat fed on cream, but unable to do a thing about it.

After a light lunch she contemplated going for a walk, and was just about to set out when she heard the sound of a car driving into the yard. From her vantage point in the kitchen she watched Miranda uncurl her slender body from the driver's seat, her face disdainful as she picked her way over the cobbled yard in spike heeled shoes. Her cream wool suit and expensive shoes were beautiful but surely completely unsuitable for farm visiting Sapphire reflected waspishly as Miranda knocked on the back door.

'If you want Blake, I'm afraid he isn't here,' she told her curtly, knowing she was being ungracious but unable to stop herself. It still hurt bitterly to think of Blake and this woman being lovers; to know that if Miranda hadn't married they still would be lovers. It did nothing to endear Miranda to her to know that at least some of Blake's desire for her must have been fuelled by the fact that he was missing *her* and Sapphire knew some of her feelings must be reflected in her face.

'It isn't Blake I wanted to see,' Miranda surprised her by saying smugly, 'Of course I knew he wouldn't be here. It's market day—we normally meet for lunch but of course since I got married. . .' She shrugged dainty shoulders. 'I've told Blake he can't have his cake and eat it. It's much pleasanter being a married woman than being a single one. . .'

'Despite the fact that you had to settle for second best,' Sapphire threw at her, regretting her impulsive comment the moment she saw the pale blue eyes harden.

'Hardly that,' Miranda drawled tautingly. 'As a lover Blake is first-rate, but as a husband?' Her eyebrows lifted. 'Hardly. For one thing Jim is an extremely wealthy man, whereas Blake. . .' She glanced round the large kitchen disparagingly. 'Being a working farmer's wife is hardly my metier. . .'

'No, I can see that,' Sapphire agreed drily, 'But

if you haven't come to see Blake why have you come here?'

Settling herself comfortably in a chair Miranda raised calculating blue eyes to Sapphire's darker ones. 'Oh I thought it was time you and I had a little talk—that er, shall we say . . . certain ground rules were laid down. You know of course that Blake and I are lovers?'

'I know you *were*,' Sapphire agreed coolly, hoping that Miranda would never guess how much the admission cost her.

'Were?' The thin eyebrows lifted tauntingly, 'Oh dear is that what he told you? And you believed him? Poor Sapphire,' she mocked. 'Blake is far too virile a man to give up what he and I have between us. Oh I grant you, you've grown up from the awkward adolescent he married, but Blake loves me, Sapphire, and all you'll ever be is a pale substitute. Your marriage to him won't last. Blake will tire of you again just like he did before.'

Her taunting words, the look in her eyes, and her own inner insecurities all combined to goad Sapphire into saying with desperate intensity, 'You're wrong; Blake wants our marriage to last.'

'You mean he wants to keep your father sweet to make sure he doesn't lose out on Flaws Farm,' Miranda derided. 'Oh come on Sapphire you know it's true. That's the only reason Blake ever married you, and the reason he wanted you back. Your father threatened to sell his farm elsewhere if he didn't. You'd better pray that he lives a long time if you're counting on seeing more than one wedding anniversary, just as Blake must be hoping that he doesn't.'

The cruelty of her gibe took Sapphire's breath

away for a moment. With tears in her eyes she cried fiercely, 'That's not true, Blake knows that my father only has a matter of months to live . . . I. . .'

'What? What on earth are you talking about?' Miranda snapped obviously disbelieving her. 'Why only last month Jim was telling me how amazed he is by your father's stamina. It must come of coming from sturdy farming stock,' she added, her lip curling fastidiously.

'Oh I know he was seriously ill with pneumonia, but Jim told me he'd never seen anyone recover so quickly from it, never mind a man well into his mid-sixties. If he's told you he's at death's door, he's lying,' she told Sapphire positively. A gleam of suspicion darkened her eyes momentarily, her gaze narrowing as she studied Sapphire with insolent appraisal. 'So that's how he got Blake to take you back,' she breathed triumphantly at last, 'by telling him that he's close to death. Of course! It would work perfectly. Poor Blake, I wonder what he's going to say when he knows he's been deceived. I can't wait to see his face,' she purred viciously. 'I don't think he's going to be too pleased about the way you've trapped him into taking you back. Oh I grant you he's single-minded enough to stay with you until he's got what he wants, but that doesn't mean he'll ever really be yours or that he cares about you.'

She turned and left before Sapphire could retaliate. Not that she had anything left to retaliate with, she thought despairingly, staring helplessly out of the window. Everything fitted together too neatly for Miranda to be wrong. She had thought herself, the last time she saw him, that her father looked better. He had even been out of bed, she remembered. Dear God how could he have done this to her? How could he have put her in this position?

Perhaps Miranda *was* wrong, she thought feverishly ... after all she had only the other woman's word for it that her father had only had pneumonia. Frantically pacing the kitchen Sapphire knew there was only one way to find out. She was already dressed for walking, so pulling on her boots she stepped out into the yard closing the kitchen door behind her.

If Miranda was right Blake would have to be told. She shivered in the cold breeze. What would his reaction be? He had never made any secret of the fact that he wanted Flaws Farm, but there was a big difference in expecting to inherit in say six months' time and waiting perhaps sixteen years? After all her grandfather had lived to his mid-eighties and so had his father before him. Walking quickly to try and blot out her jumbled thoughts, Sapphire headed for Flaws Farm.

CHAPTER TEN

'YOUR father?' Mary responded in answer to Sapphire's query. 'Yes, he's in his room.'

'How is he today?' Sapphire watched closely as she waited for Mary's response.

'Oh much better,' the older woman beamed. 'In fact he's improving rapidly every day now. As soon as this cold spell breaks he'll probably be able to go outside. He's chaffing at the bit now I'm afraid,' she smiled ruefully, 'not the best of patients, but then that's understandable when one thinks of the active life he's led.'

'But he will be able to get out and about?' Sapphire queried.

'Good heavens yes.' Mary looked surprised that she even needed to ask. 'Pneumonia is serious of course, but these days, with modern drugs, its not dangerous, and of course your father is supremely fit.'

'Pneumonia. . . There weren't any other complications then?' Sapphire asked trying to sound casual while inwardly shaking with dread. So Miranda *had* been right after all.

'Not as far as I know.' Mary looked concerned. 'I know you must be worried about him, but there really is no need you know,' she told her gently. 'For a while he did seem to have reached a plateau stage, but since you came back he's really made progress. I suspect the hope of a grandchild has had some bearing on that. Men hereabouts place a great deal of importance on continuance of the family line. I think when your father was ill he brooded rather a lot on the fact that he was the last male Bell, but he's definitely over that now. Why don't you go up and see him, he'll welcome the interruption. He's working on the farm accounts.' She grinned conspiratorily, 'And you know how he hates that.'

It was amazing what one could see when one knew what to look for Sapphire thought wretchedly, opening the door without knocking and walking into a scene familiar to her from her childhood.

Her father's dog lay curled up at his feet, swear words turning the air mildly blue as he bent his head over his ledgers. Seeing him now with her new knowledge, Sapphire could see that he had been ill and that he was recovering. There was more flesh on his bones for one thing and for another the colour of his skin was better. The door creaked faintly as she let it swing closed and he turned round, his welcoming smile changing to a frown as he saw her pale face.

'Sapphire.' He got up, coming towards her, but she avoided him, sitting down in a spare chair.

'I know exactly what's been going on, Dad,' she said quietly. 'I know you're not . . . not dying. Her control broke as she cried out wretchedly, 'How could you do this to me . . .? How could you trick and deceive . . .?'

'Lass, lass, believe me I thought it best,' he interrupted sadly. 'Your place is here with your husband. I've always thought that.'

'You're free to think what you like, Dad, but to try to force me back with Blake by pretending. . .'

She bit her lip, turning away from the remorse in his face.

'Sapphire, perhaps I shouldn't have meddled, but believe me I thought it was for the best. It was plain to me that you weren't happy in London. You loved Blake when you married him.'

'But he didn't love me, he only married me to get Flaws Farm. That's the only reason he took me back,' she cried wildly. 'Can't you see that? He doesn't really want me, he only wants your land, and the only reason he re-married me was because he thought it wouldn't be long before he inherited it. We made a bargain you see,' she told him wretchedly, 'peace of mind for you, and Flaws Farm for Blake. I agreed I'd sell it to him, once... How do you suppose he'll feel when he discovers how you've tricked him and he *will* discover it...'

'Sapphire, you've got it all wrong,' her father interrupted sternly. 'I've never deceived Blake. He knew exactly what was wrong with me. He wanted you back here as much as I did. Don't you see ... Blake knew the truth ... he knew, Sapphire...'

For a few minutes it was too much for her to take in and then she burst out bitterly, 'I see ... and how were the pair of you planning to resolve this grand charade—a miracle recovery? And to think I fell for it.' Unable to endure any more she wrenched open the door, ignoring her father's anguished cry, half-running through the kitchen and out into the yard. The afternoon was drawing in and the cold blast of air against her heated skin stung, but Sapphire ignored it, head down, hands stuffed into her pockets as she walked doggedly away from the farm, instinctively taking the path that had been her favourite as a child.

It led to a disused quarry, now overgrown and mossy. As a child she had discovered a moss-covered ledge halfway down one of the escarpments, and almost hidden from view by the lip of the quarry.

This had been a favourite refuge of her childhood, and now driven by an intense need to be alone she automatically took the path that led to it.

She could understand what her father had had to gain from deceiving her, but Blake. . . Had her father perhaps dangled the farm in front of him? Take Sapphire back, give me a grandchild and in return. . . Her mind shied away from the thought. No, Blake would never allow himself to be manoeuvred like that, he wasn't that type of man, but he was very fond of her father . . . and he did want Flaws' land . . . and he did find her desirable. Given that might he not decide that marriage to her was a reasonable price to pay, especially when he could still be Miranda's lover?

Round and round her thoughts circled, tormenting her with each combination that came to mind. There were so many imponderables for her to consider, so many differing combinations, and only Blake knew the real truth; exactly what had motivated him. But now it would have to end. She couldn't stay with him knowing what she now did. Humiliation seared her soul when she thought about their lovemaking; about the intensity of emotion she had put into it when he had merely been enduring it out of necessity.

On and on she walked, scarcely aware that it

was starting to get dark, setting one foot in front of the other, wrestling with her thoughts.

By the time she reached the quarry it was almost dark, but logic and common sense had long since given way to an instinct for sanctuary which led her to seek out the treacherous path going down to her childhood hiding place.

She found it more by instinct than anything else, stumbling once halfway down and clinging to the quarry face for support as a tiny avalanche of stones crumbled downwards beneath her feet, to eventually splash eerily into the deep pool that had formed at the centre of the quarry crater. This place had been out of bounds to her as a child but it had never stopped her coming here. She shivered suddenly, coming out of the bleak despair that had driven her to seek out this place, swaying lightheadedly. Perhaps she ought to go back; her father would be worrying about her. Remorse overcame her earlier anger. Of course he had been doing what he thought best; to him no doubt she was still the shy seventeen-year-old who had first fallen in love with Blake. And her father *was* old-fashioned. To him marriage vows were sacrosanct and not lightly to be set aside. Sighing faintly Sapphire started to turn round, freezing tensely as she felt the shale beneath her feet shift. The last time she had come down here she had been seventeen—a child bride looking for somewhere to escape the miseries of a marriage that had turned out to be so far removed from her childish imaginings of high romance that now it seemed to be a farce. Even then the path had been dangerous—something she had forgotten when she came down it tonight. She shivered again remembering the remoteness of the quarry and the unlikelihood of anyone guessing that she was up here. If she made it to the ledge she would be stuck there until morning when she might be able to attract the attention of one of the shepherds. If she made it, she thought wretchedly as another part of the path slid away to drop into the pool. The pool. Icy trickles of fear dripped down her spine. The water in that pool was freezing, its sides smooth and worn by time into a glassy slipperiness that made the pool a death trap for anyone foolish enough to swim in it. Closing her eyes and clinging to the wall of the quarry she inched her way carefully down to the ledge, easing her shaking body on to its grassy smoothness.

It seemed smaller than she remembered and as she edged back against the quarry wall, trying to sit down she realised why. Like the path, the ledge had been partially eroded away. Every time she moved she could hear the rattling of shale and small stones. How safe was the ledge? She could die here and no-one would be any the wiser. Would it matter if she did? Was life really worth living without Blake? If one judged life on its quality rather than its quantity then no. Without him her life had no direction; no purpose. Without his love... Wearily her body relaxed into a numbing lethargy that was almost a relief, her mind torturing her with images of Blake and on to the point where death lured her with its promise of oblivion.

Suicide had always been something she had viewed with horror—until she lost Blake, and now with sharp clarity she remembered those first months after she had left him, when she would have given anything not to have had to wake up in the morning. Now she was going to lose him again. The moon slid out from behind a cloud illuminating the still water below. It beckoned to her, casting a spell that seemed to reach out and enfold her until she could almost imagine she was already in its icy embrace. As though obeying the directions of a voice only she could hear Sapphire stood up, drifting like a sleep-walker towards the edge of the ledge where she stood poised, drawn by the inky black depths below, her powers of reasoning clouded by the greater force of her emotions.

'No!'

At first Sapphire thought the taut cry had been torn from her own throat, but when it was followed by her name, called abruptly by a familiar male voice she started back from the edge of the ledge, staring up in disbelief to find Blake looking down at her.

Perhaps it was a trick of the moonlight, but his face seemed oddly white and drawn, his eyes burning as though he had looked into the fires of hell.

'Stand back from the edge Sapphire, and I'll throw you down a rope.'

She was too bemused to question how he had got there, simply obeying the commands he shouted down to her, feeling the coarse fibre of the rope bite into her waist as Blake hauled her back up the quarry face, until she was lying flat on her back, on the ice-cold grass, breathing in great gulps of air, like a landed fish.

Blake's fingers tugged at the knotted rope, unfastening it from around her. His head bent over his self-imposed task, Sapphire resisted the urge to reach out and stroke the thick darkness, but she couldn't restrain the brief quiver tensing her body when she remembered how they had made love.

'Keep still,' Blake's voice was terse, his hands clinically detached as they examined her body. 'Nothing seems to be broken... Come on, I'd better get you back and alert the rest of the team.' As she stood up Sapphire saw that his mouth was compressed, his eyes darkly bitter as they studied her.

'The team?' Was that really her own voice, soft and husky almost begging him to reach out and touch her?

'The Rescue Team,' he reminded her in the same clipped voice. 'Your father called them out when you didn't come back. Tom Barnes rang me and asked me to stand in for Geoff Plant—he's away at the moment. I had no idea when I set out that it was you...' He broke off and turned away from her, rubbing his forehead with tense fingers. 'I called at Flaws on the way to see if you were there—I thought you might have decided to spend the evening with your father...'

'In view of his ailing health I suppose you mean,' Sapphire cut in sarcastically, only to be silenced by Blake's brusque, 'Not now Sapphire. You realise your father's practically frantic with worry, to say nothing of how I felt...'

'And how did you feel Blake?' she asked bitterly, suddenly furiously and intensely angry, the adrenalin flowing fiercely along her veins. 'Worried that you might not get Flaws after all? Oh yes, I know all about how the pair of you deceived me. Your very good friend Miranda enlightened me. My father I can forgive because I know he acted in what he believed to be my best interests, but you...' Her heated words were silenced by the brief blast Blake gave on the whistle he was holding.

'We can discuss all that later,' he told her curtly. 'Right now, like the rest of the team, all I want to do is get home to bed. You do realise that if I hadn't remembered about this damned quarry, you'd have been there until morning, if not longer, don't you? And just what the hell were you playing at when I arrived, for God's sake?' he shouted at her, fingers clenching into her shoulders as he shook her roughly. Once given life it seemed as though his anger couldn't be quenched, and Sapphire listened in silence as it flowed moltenly over her. Blake was angry... It was a phenomenon she had never witnessed before. Before he had always been so cool and in control.

Other members of the team alerted by his whistle were hurrying towards them, and he stopped berating her, turning instead to assure them that she was quite safe.

'She slipped off the path and luckily for her landed on a ledge,' was the explanation he gave his co-rescuers, and after Sapphire had endured some well-deserved chaffing on the subject of her carelessness Blake started to guide her towards where he had left his Land Rover.

'I'll call at Flaws and let Simon have the good news,' one of the men offered. 'It's on my way, and you'll both be wanting to get back home. Hot baths and a good mug of toddy, put the pair of you to rights. . .' He winked over his shoulder at Blake, and Sapphire felt the warmth seep up under her skin as she intercepted the very male look they exchanged. And the worst of it was that deep down inside her she still yearned for Blake to take her into the warmth of his bed and hold her until all the nightmare details of the day faded into oblivion.

Instead she had to sit with him in the Land Rover, the tense quality of the silence stretching between them acting on her nerves with all the torment of a thumbscrew. When the Land Rover eventually came to a halt in the farmyard she was out the moment Blake cut the engine, shocked to discover how weak her legs felt as she clung wretchedly to her open door.

'You should have waited for me.' The terse, unsympathetic words brought tears of weakness and pain to her eyes, but thankfully it was too dark for Blake to see them. She wanted to protest when he walked round to her and hauled her carelessly into his arms, but she knew that she just didn't have the strength to object.

Upstairs she lay on the bed where he had dropped her knowing that she couldn't endure sleeping with him now. Not that he was likely to want to. Her mouth twisted bitterly. Had he, like her father, hoped they might have a child— preferably a son who could inherit the rich Flaws acres he coveted? Was that why. . . Unable to endure the torment of her thoughts she gave a low moan, rolling on to her stomach.

'Can you manage to get undressed or. . .'

Until Blake spoke she had forgotten she was still wearing her outdoor clothes.

'I can manage.' Her voice was colourless and completely dry.

'Sapphire, we have to talk.'

Was that uncertainty and pain she could hear threading through the determined words? Anger hardened her heart. Whatever he might be enduring through guilt and fear of losing Flaws was nothing compared with her own agony. 'Tomorrow,' she told him briefly. 'I don't want to talk tonight Blake . . . I need to think.' It was a lie, but at least it got him out of her room.

When he had gone she struggled exhaustedly to remove her clothes, almost crawling into the bathroom. Her legs were bruised and scraped where they had rubbed against the rough stone of the quarry walls, the abrasions stinging with the hot water. Bathed and dried she went back into the bedroom, tensing as she saw Blake waiting there.

'I already told you, I don't want to talk tonight Blake,' she told him rudely. 'I'm tired, and so if you don't mind. . .' Glad that she had had the forethought to take her nightdress into the bathroom with her, she swept past him with magnificent disdain, hoping that he wouldn't guess how vulnerable and hurt she was really feeling.

'It's a bit late for this isn't it?' Lean fingers reached out and tugged at the fine lawn fabric. 'After last night. . .'

'Last night is something that should never have happened and would never have happened if I'd known. . .' Sapphire gasped out loud as Blake's fingers moved from the frill of her nightdress to the vee of its neckline, stroking softly over the upper swell of her breasts.

'You think not?' Blake's voice was soft, almost detached, but there was nothing detached about the look in his eyes Sapphire realised, her heart starting to thud with powerful, heavy thuds. 'I'm getting tired of playing "let's make believe", Sapphire,' Blake told her thickly. 'Last night you wanted me, and tonight I could make you want me again.'

'No!' The harsh denial was out before she could stop it and the moment it was said Sapphire knew she had made a mistake. It was almost as though something snapped inside Blake, some fine thread whose snapping unleashed a savage tumult of emotions that demanded expression.

Her moaned protest of 'Blake you can't do this', went unheard as he picked her up and carried her over to the bed, stripping off her nightdress with ruthless, hard fingers, his touch a thousand times removed from that of the tender lover of the previous night.

'I know you want me, damn you,' Blake muttered in a tortured whisper against her skin, bruising it faintly with the pressure of lips suddenly savage with pent-up emotions whose origins she could only guess at. His thumb brushed her nipple and Sapphire felt the unmistakable flowering of her body, her cry of despair mingling with Blake's murmured triumph.

As he bent his head to touch her treacherous body first with his tongue and then his lips Sapphire felt the first weak tears of broken pride slide from her eyes. In the darkness Blake lifted his head and stared at her, his thumb touching the dampness of her face.

'You're crying. Why?' If she hadn't known

better Sapphire might have believed that the pain in his voice was real; that the anguish in his eyes was because he couldn't bear to hurt her, but she did know better. She turned her head away from him too weak to stem the tears.

'Don't touch me Blake,' she begged huskily, 'Please . . . just leave me alone.'

She closed her eyes and felt the bed shift under his weight. When she opened them again he had gone.

Sleep was a long time coming. She could hear Blake moving about in his own room; the noises of the old house as it settled into sleep disturbing tonight instead of vaguely comforting. Tomorrow she would have to tell Blake she was leaving him. No running away this time. She would tell him this time that she was going, and that she was never going to come back. A sob stuck in her throat and suddenly she was crying as she could not remember doing in a long time, tearing, painful sobs that left her chest aching and her eyes sore.

'Sapphire, are you awake?'

Slowly she turned her head. Blake was standing just inside the door, his hair ruffled and on edge, his shirt half-unfastened, a cup of tea in one hand. 'I've brought you a drink,' he told her unnecessarily when she lifted her head from the pillow.

'What time is it?' Sapphire glanced at her watch, dismayed to see that it was midmorning. 'Shouldn't you be out working?'

It was obviously the wrong thing to say. Blake's mouth thinned, anger hardening his eyes. 'It's all right,' she muttered huskily. 'This time I'm not

going to run away. This time when I leave. . .'
She broke off stunned by the sudden blaze of heat
turning his eyes molten gold, which died just as
quickly when she started to finish her sentence.
Surely Blake couldn't want her to stay? Not for
herself, she told herself cynically, but perhaps for
the farm. The thought sickened her as it had done
ever since it had first come into her mind all those
years ago.

'I'd better get up.'

'Sapphire we have to talk.' Blake's voice
sounded thick and hoarse, and now that she
looked at him properly she saw that beneath the
healthy tan of his face he looked drawn and tired.

'We can talk downstairs,' she told him reason-
ably, feeling very much at a disadvantage in bed
while he stood, virtually fully dressed, in front of
her. She hadn't put another nightdress on after he
had left her and the remnants of the one he had
torn off her body lay on the floor at her side of the
bed.

'No, now. . .' One stride brought him alongside
the bed, the mattress dipping under his weight as
he sat down next to her, one lean arm imprisoning
her against his side should she have any thoughts
of trying to turn away.

'All right . . .' he admitted tiredly when she said
nothing. 'I know I shouldn't have done it . . .
you've every reason to hate me for it, God knows,
I knew when your father suggested it that it was a
crazy idea, but then when a man's as desperate as I
was, any idea, no matter how crazy, has its
appeal.'

'My forebears would be extremely flattered to
know how eager you are to gain possession of

Flaws' land,' Sapphire gritted at him. 'Such a noble sacrifice. . .' Some demon she had never suspected she possessed drove her on. '. . . even to the extent of giving up your mistress, but then that wouldn't have lasted would it? How long did you intend to devote your attentions to me? Long enough to get me pregnant—to provide my father with a grandson? And we both know what a sacrifice that would have been, don't we Blake? I should have remembered how much you loathed touching me, instead of deluding myself into. . .' She broke off as Blake wrenched the bedclothes away, squirming away from him, trying to cover her naked breasts by folding her arms.

'So I loathe touching you do I?' Blake muttered huskily, tugging her arms away from her body and then cupping the rounded warmth of her breasts stroking their pink tips with rough thumb pads. A deep sensual warmth burgeoned somewhere deep within her, increasing in intensity when she felt the fine tremor in Blake's hands. His eyes golden and fiery as the sun seemed to bathe her skin in molten heat, the expression she saw in their glowing depths as he bent his head to touch his lips first to one pink nipple and then the other making her wonder if she had suddenly completely lost her wits. 'Does this feel like I loathe the enticement of your skin beneath my fingers?' Blake demanded rawly releasing her breasts to spread brown hands possessively against her rib cage. 'Or this.' Hot damp kisses filled the valley between her breasts, his lips exploring the tender column of her throat, teasing the line of her jaw, his teeth nipping delicately at the fullness of her bottom lip until her lips parted and the fine tremor of his body became an open spasm of need, his mouth savagely hungry as it possessed hers, his tongue pushing past her teeth to explore its inner sweetness.

Unable to stop herself Sapphire caressed the firm muscles under his skin, stroking his neck and shoulders and feeling the powerful surge of his body's response.

'I love you so much,' Blake whispered as he lifted his mouth from hers, touching its swollen contours with his tongue as though unable to stop himself from doing so, 'that's my only defence. I nearly went crazy when you left me, hoping that you'd come back, telling myself that I'd find a way to get you back, and then when your father told me you were thinking of marrying again. . .' She felt him swallow and saw the unmistakable truth darkening his eyes, shining in the unexpected tears that shimmered in his eyes.

'You love me?' She could hardly trust herself to say the words. How could that be true?

'Always,' he averred.

'But you never made love to me, never. . .'

'Because you were so young,' he told her abruptly. 'Because I knew I'd taken advantage of what was little more than an infatuation, using it to bind you to me when you'd barely had a chance to taste real life.'

'I thought you didn't want me.'

'Not want you.' He closed his eyes, and swallowed hard. 'I wanted you so much I couldn't trust myself within a hundred yards of you, but I wanted you as a man wants the woman he loves Sapphire, not as an adolescent boy wants the first girl he falls in love with. I was terrified of frightening you away, and yet I knew that once I touched you I wouldn't be able to control myself; that I couldn't play the controlled lover. . .'

'And that was why you went to Miranda?' she asked in a low voice.

'I never "went to her" as you put it. Once, a long time before I fell in love with you she and I were lovers, but never since. . .'

'But the other night. . .'

'I wanted to make you jealous. To make you feel the same agony as I've endured over Alan. I spent the entire evening driving around in my car. After you'd gone out I rang her back cancelling the date.'

'But you wrote her love letters,' Sapphire told him, frowning as she remembered finding that incriminating evidence.

'Love letters?' Blake stared down at her.

'Yes.' Pain ached through her, her eyes clouding. 'When my father told me you married me because you wanted the farm, and after I'd seen what you'd written, I knew I couldn't stay . . . I saw the letter myself Blake, it was so full of . . . of need and love. . .' She couldn't go on, remembering as though it had been yesterday how she had felt.

Suddenly Blake's frown cleared. 'Stay here,' he told her softly. 'Don't move.'

He was gone less than five minutes, during which time she had pulled the bedclothes back up round her body, but the first thing Blake did when he walked back into the room was to pull them down again. 'I love looking at your body,' he told her simply. 'It makes up for all the years when I couldn't. You can't imagine how I felt when I found out you were still a virgin.' His lips caressed one deeply pink peak, bringing it achingly to life, and then as though unable to resist the temptation, transferred to the other, adoration giving way to passionate need as he felt her body's unmistakable response and Sapphire arched achingly, longing to curl her fingers into his hair and hold him against her, but the paper he had dropped on the bed caught her eye and she tensed, causing him to stop and pull her into the warmth of his body so that she was leaning against his thighs her head cushioned against his shoulder.

'Is this what you read?' he asked her gently, offering her the close written sheets. Sapphire only needed to read the first few words to nod an assent.

'And because of this you left me? Oh! Sapphire...' His voice broke and she felt the damp warmth of his tears against her skin. 'I wrote them for *you*,' he told her brokenly, 'I wrote what I daren't tell you! What I couldn't in all honour show you... You're the only woman I've ever loved and when I saw you standing on that ledge, about to go over into the pool, I didn't know what I wanted to do most—strangle you or strangle Alan for hurting you so much that you felt you needed to end your life because of him.'

'It wasn't him, it was you,' Sapphire told him urgently. Right now it was almost impossible to take in the enormity of what had happened; but that Blake was telling the truth when he said he loved her she didn't for one moment doubt.

'After Miranda told me the truth about my father's illness I knew I couldn't stay with you—not when really you loved her, and yet I didn't know where I was going to find the courage to leave, loving you so much.'

'I've never loved anyone but you,' Blake interrupted fiercely. 'I think you were all of sixteen years' old the first time I realised how I felt about you. Miranda lied to you.'

Because she had been jealous, Sapphire now realised, but she had been clever as well, using her sophistication and experience to drive a wedge between them, no doubt hoping that Blake would turn to her once Sapphire had left him.

'So many wasted years,' she said sadly raising bleak eyes to meet his.

'No . . . not wasted. You *were* too young for marriage at seventeen,' Blake told her. 'I would always have felt guilty and uncertain wondering if I had stolen from you the right to make your own choice of husband, but now I know that you love *me*. You do love me, don't you?' he demanded thickly, when Sapphire remained silent.

Part of her longed to tease him just a little, but the rest of her responded eagerly to the plea in his eyes, her body curling into his as she kissed him, lightly at first and then with growing need, breaking away from him only to murmur huskily, 'So much. . . Blake if you hadn't arrived at the quarry when you did. . .' A shudder wracked her body and she felt him tense in response. 'Don't,' he commanded her rawly. 'Don't even think about it, just tell me you've forgiven me for lying to you about your father. I hated myself for doing it; for causing you pain—a pain I could see every time you looked at your father, but I was desperate to get you back; willing to do anything to stop you from marrying someone else.'

'And having got me back how did you intend to keep me?' Sapphire teased, forgiveness explicit in the look she gave him as she reached out to push the unruly hair back off his forehead.

'Oh, I'd have thought of something.' The old assurance was creeping back into his voice, but she didn't mind. Now that she had seen his vulnerability she could accept the macho side of his personality more easily. 'Such as?' she whispered, feathering light kisses along his jaw and glorying in his responsive shudder.

'Such as this ... and this...' Blake's voice deepened, raw need underlying the husky words as he caressed her body, kissing her silky skin, words no longer necessary.

Now she really had come home, Sapphire thought contentedly abandoning herself completely into his keeping, revelling in the fierce thrust of pleasure seizing his body as he recognised her surrender, and she was never ever going to leave again. Closing her eyes she murmured the words of love she knew he longed to hear, for the first time saying them in complete trust that she would hear them back in return.

'The stock ...' she reminded Blake weakly long, satisfying minutes later. . . 'You. . .'

'To hell with the stock,' Blake responded thickly. 'Right now I've got far more important things on my mind, like making love to my wife, unless of course she has any objections?'

A smile dimpled the corner of Sapphire's mouth. 'Only one,' she told him gravely, 'and that is that you're wasting far too much time in talk instead of action. . .'

Retaliation was every bit as swift as she had envisaged—and every bit as pleasurable, the words of love she had longed to hear for so long caressing her skin in silken whispers as Blake took her back in his arms.

Here's how to get this special offer from Harlequin!
As simple as 1…2…3!

AUGUST
TREASURY EDITION
COUPON

1. Each month, save one Treasury Edition coupon from your favorite Romance or Presents novel.
2. In four months you'll have saved four Treasury Edition coupons (<u>only one coupon per month allowed</u>).
3. Then all you have to do is fill out and return the order form provided, along with the four Treasury Edition coupons required and $1.00 for postage and handling.

Mail to: Harlequin Reader Service

RT1-A-2

In the U.S.A.
P.O. Box 52040
Phoenix, AZ 85072-2040

In Canada
P.O. Box 2800, Postal Station A
5170 Yonge Street
Willowdale, Ont. M2N 6J3

Please send me my FREE copy of the Janet Dailey Treasury Edition. I have enclosed the four Treasury Edition coupons required and $1.00 for postage and handling along with this order form.

(Please Print)

NAME_____

ADDRESS_____

CITY_____

STATE/PROV. _____ ZIP/POSTAL CODE_____

SIGNATURE_____

This offer is limited to one order per household.

SUPPLIES LIMITED

This special Janet Dailey offer expires January 1986.

EYE OF THE STORM

MAURA SEGER

A powerful
portrayal of
the events of
World War II in the
Pacific, *Eye of the Storm* is a riveting story of how love
triumphs over hatred. In this, the first of a three-book
chronicle, Army nurse Maggie Lawrence meets Marine
Sgt. Anthony Gargano. Despite military regulations
against fraternization, they resolve to face together
whatever lies ahead.... Author Maura Seger, also known
to her fans as Laurel Winslow, Sara Jennings, Anne
MacNeil and Jenny Bates, was named 1984's
Most Versatile Romance Author by *The Romantic Times*

You're invited to accept 4 books and a surprise gift **Free!**

Acceptance Card

Mail to: Harlequin Reader Service®

In the U.S.
2504 West Southern Ave.
Tempe, AZ 85282

In Canada
P.O. Box 2800, Postal Station A
5170 Yonge Street
Willowdale, Ontario M2N 6J3

YES! Please send me 4 free Harlequin Presents® novels and my free surprise gift. Then send me 8 brand new novels every month as they come off the presses. Bill me at the low price of $1.75 each ($1.95 in Canada) — an 11% saving off the retail price. There are no shipping, handling or other hidden costs. There is no minimum number of books I must purchase. I can always return a shipment and cancel at any time. Even if I never buy another book from Harlequin, the 4 free novels and the surprise gift are mine to keep forever.

108 BPP-BPGE

Name _____ (PLEASE PRINT)

Address _____ Apt. No. _____

City _____ State/Prov. _____ Zip/Postal Code _____

This offer is limited to one order per household and not valid to present subscribers. Price is subject to change.

ACP-SUB-1

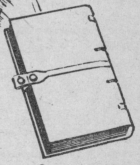